HEARTWARMING DESIGNS

A BABY CHANGES EVERYTHING

CARMEN KLASSEN

Heartwarming Designs

CONTENTS

CHAPTER 1

*J*az lay motionless in her bed, breathing as shallow as possible. As soon as she heard the front door close, she jumped up and dashed to the bathroom. Kneeling in front of the toilet she threw up. Tears streamed down her face as she felt her body continue to retch. She wasn't stupid. This probably meant the worst thing that could possibly happen. Jasmine Lee, only child, class valedictorian, on the starting line of her volleyball team, and set to start pre-med in September, was pregnant.

She lay down on the cold tile floor for a few minutes before making herself get up. Opening the window and turning on the fan, she got in the shower and sat down. It was too hard to stay standing while her legs were shaking. At exactly 6:45 her mom would return from her morning run, and Jaz would pretend that everything was fine.

Final exams started next week. Then graduation, and the valedictorian speech she had already written and memorized—before realizing she had ruined everything. After another minute of crying in the shower, she forced herself to stop. Her mom couldn't possibly guess what was wrong, but she'd know that something wasn't right if she came downstairs with red eyes.

Jaz had three things to do today: survive school, go to a walk-in clinic and get a pregnancy test, and hide everything from her parents. No matter what happened next, she would give them their moment to bask in the glory of having a brilliant, popular daughter who was going to be a surgeon before she destroyed their whole world by making one very big mistake. And if she wasn't pregnant, then at least her parents would never know that she had slept with their best friend's 'perfect' son.

As an x-ray technician her mom left the house at 7:25 every morning, leaving Jaz a chance to be sick once more if she needed before leaving to go to school. Since her parents monitored her movements throughout the day, she had to make it to school on time. The first time she was sick she thought it was the flu, so she had stayed home. But when her mom arrived home after work and saw she was fine, she accused her of just being lazy. The next day Jaz forced herself to go to school but spent the first hour in the girls' bathroom.

At least volleyball season was over, so she had an excuse to go straight home after school. She usually went to bed, but was always careful to set an alarm and be at the table studying when her mom came in from work at 4:35. Dinner was always at 5:30.

Her parents insisted she not work during school, but she *was* expected to try to find a summer job. Jaz had sent out over thirty resumes already with no response. The economy had forced many adults to apply for most of the jobs students normally held, and students were now bumped to the end of the line for any available positions.

But worries about a summer job might be the least of her problems. Hopefully they would tell her at the clinic that everything was normal and she could go back to pleasing her parents.

After school Jaz said good-bye to her friends before turning off her phone and walking to the clinic. If her parents asked, she'd claim the battery died. She had used the school computer to look up clinics within walking distance. All of her friends had doctors in fancy

2

offices downtown, so she wasn't worried about running into anyone as she walked into a run-down office in a strip mall.

When she explained to the receptionist that she thought she was pregnant, she was sent to give a urine sample before being shown into a room. The time passed slowly as she waited, but she wouldn't dare turn her phone on. She looked down at her white jeans, and brushed an imaginary speck off of them. Paired with a chambray button-up shirt, and with a cardigan perfectly draped around her shoulders, she looked like a typical over-achieving only child. With all her heart she hoped she would still be that girl after the appointment. Finally, a lady came in.

"Hi there, Jasmine?"

"Yeah, I go by Jaz."

"Hi, I'm Kara, the physician's assistant. You're here for a pregnancy test?"

Jaz nodded and pointed to the sample she had placed on the counter. The lady washed her hands and put on gloves. She was wearing a lab coat covered in rainbows over a bright yellow blouse, dark skinny jeans, and tan ankle boots. Jaz thought she looked like a snapshot of the sky to the earth.

After looking at the test strip she took off her gloves and washed her hands again before turning around with a smile and sitting in the chair across from Jaz. "You're right. It's a strong positive. You're pregnant."

Jaz tried to say something, but when she opened her mouth, nothing came out.

"I'm guessing this wasn't your plan."

Jaz shook her head no, and felt tears start to fill her eyes. She looked down at her hands clenched in her lap.

"How old are you?"

"Eighteen," Jaz whispered.

"OK, so you're set to graduate in a few weeks?"

Again, she nodded in reply.

"Would you like to hear about some options?"

Jaz shook her head 'no'. "I know them. Adoption, abortion, keep." It felt strange to say them out loud. Like she was admitting to being a different person than who she thought she was. If it wasn't for the morning sickness, she wouldn't believe she was pregnant—despite what the lady had just told her.

"OK. Why don't you focus on graduating for now, and make your decision after that? There's no rush, except that I do recommend you begin taking a prenatal vitamin. My name's Kara. If you have any questions or need anything you can come back here and talk to me."

Jaz finally looked up. Kara acted like this was so normal. It was the worst thing she could imagine happening to her, and yet this lady seemed so calm and nonjudgmental. When she smiled, Jaz couldn't help but timidly smile back. "Thanks."

"You're welcome. Remember, I'm here if you need anything."

Jaz made it home in time to turn her phone back on and set up her books at the table in the dining room before her mom came home. She forced herself to practice chemistry equations until she was called for supper. As usual, her dad would be home later and would eat alone.

CHAPTER 2

The morning after her graduation Jaz couldn't wait until her mom left the house before she was sick. Blaming it on the late night, she went back to bed after and waited for the nausea to pass, praying that her mom wouldn't check on her. As she lay there, she thought about the ceremony and dinner afterwards.

It had been her parent's crowning moment. Having their daughter as the valedictorian, bragging about her acceptance to university, comparing life plans with other parents. There were moments when she forgot she was pregnant and chattered happily with the other kids her parents approved of—all smart, hard-working, and on their way to university either this fall or next if they were taking the socially acceptable gap year.

But then reality would hit, and she'd force herself to pretend to be happy when her insides were dissolving in anxiety and sadness. The worst was talking to Ellison. After that one night together, they hadn't talked about what had happened. She thought there might be something—a special look, or maybe he'd ask her out or something. But he hadn't changed how he treated her at all. His parents were telling everyone about his place at MIT, and Jaz had to clench her teeth at the unfairness of it all. No matter what happened next, he wouldn't be affected like she was.

Worried about what her parents would say when she told them she was pregnant, she thought it would be easier to tell Ellison first. When she was mostly sure she could start her day, she texted him:

I need to talk to you today. Meet at Connie's?

Connie's was a café where the 'good' kids would go for milkshakes and fries. It was only a few blocks from the school, but since it was expensive it catered to a certain crowd. One that people like Jaz and Ellison were used to belonging to. Hours later, he responded:

Sure, 3? I'm shopping with my mom right now.

Jaz rolled her eyes. The only mom more concerned about image than her mom was Ellison's. He always dressed like he was on his way to a photo shoot for a magazine ad. Everything about him looked perfect—at least on the outside. She knew her parents hoped that one day the two of them would get together. Maybe because the baby was Ellison's it would make it easier to tell them. She texted back that three was good and then tried to fill the time until then applying for jobs.

Her parents were covering all her expenses for university, so she didn't really need to work, but she wanted to because that's what they expected of her now. They never let her have a part-time job while she was in school, and last summer she had spent her time volunteering at the hospital to improve her college application. But now that she was accepted, she didn't need to volunteer anymore.

Finally, it was time to go meet Ellison. She texted her mom about where she was going and who she was meeting, and then left to walk the twenty minutes to Connie's. In her tan walking shorts and white polo shirt with white sandals, she hoped she looked like the type of person he wanted. He was already there when she arrived, with a milkshake in front of him. Jaz's breath caught for a minute.

Ellison was tall, with perfectly styled dark hair, perfect clothes, and a perfect body — something that she knew personally now. He was also wearing tan walking shorts, but with a pink polo shirt and tan loafers with no socks.

"Hey, got over your big night last night?" He smiled big before taking a drink from his milkshake.

"Uh yeah, thanks." She shook her head 'no' when the waitressed started to walk over. She was too nervous to think about eating. It looked like Ellison had already ordered something, since there was a full place setting in front of him.

"So, what's up?" He was so confident and sure of himself.

"You know… that night. When we were supposed to study," she felt herself blushing just thinking about it.

"Yeah, we were pretty hot, hey? I mean, like, if you were going to MIT too, we could hook up. There's always the summer though. But I'm not looking for anything serious. Just some fun, right?"

"I'm pregnant!" she blurted out. And then slapped her hand over her mouth and looked around. Hopefully no one had heard her.

"What? No way!" He leaned forward and lowered his voice. "That's not possible! You can't be …*that*."

"I checked with a doctor. I am." She watched his face carefully. Disbelief quickly turned to shock, but then he smiled and reached for her hand.

"Don't worry. We can take care of this. Jamieson knows this clinic. I can find out and get you in. I'll pay for everything too. Nobody will know."

She tried to process what he was saying. Jamieson was his best friend, but he had a reputation for getting around. Jaz's mom had always warned her about Jamieson and other 'white boys' who would take advantage of her if she let them.

"I, um, no. I don't think that's what I want. Maybe adoption—"

"—Oh my God, Jaz. Don't be stupid. Nobody will want to adopt an Asian baby. And you can't let anyone know. My parents would kill me, and so would yours. This needs to end! You can't go to university pregnant! What were you thinking?"

She felt tears pooling in her eyes. This was not what she was expecting.

"Listen, it's up to you. You know, it's your body and all that. But you have to keep me out of it." He stopped abruptly as the waitress came and put an order of chili cheese fries in front of him.

"What can I get you?"

"Oh, um, nothing thank you." Jaz watched her walk away. She looked around the café, trying to figure out what to say next. But Ellison seemed to have recovered from her announcement.

"If you need money or anything I can totally help. Just don't tell anyone it's me. You know my parents wouldn't believe it anyways. So that would just make you look bad, right? You know, your reputation is for forever. Just, um…text me if you need anything. But don't say why. You know, in case my mom sees my phone."

Jaz sat there watching him eat his fries as if he didn't have a problem in the world. Finally, she stood up and walked away. She was pretty sure she heard him call 'see ya later'. For the next hour she walked the streets around her neighborhood, trying to figure out what to do. When she decided to go home she still didn't know.

CHAPTER 3

For the next few weeks Jaz struggled to make it through each day. She hid in bed until her mom left for work, waited out the nausea, and then spent the afternoons walking. Sometimes she'd see friends, but she no longer shared their excitement about the future.

Feeling like she was missing out she finally agreed to meet a group at the park. If she could just forget about being pregnant for one afternoon, it would be the mental break she needed. She tried to gossip with the others but it seemed so pointless. It didn't help that Ellison was there too, laughing, and flirting. Finally one of the girls called her on it, "Geez, you're never any fun anymore. What's your problem?"

Jaz stared at her for a minute, wondering whether to tell the truth. She glanced at Ellison but he didn't seem to notice her dilemma. Behind him, a girl she barely recognized from high school walked by, pushing a stroller.

"Slut!" Shocked, Jaz turned to Sherry, the girl she considered one of her closest friends.

"You don't know that," Jaz whispered.

"Are you kidding? Any girl *stupid* enough to get pregnant nowadays is definitely a slut."

Jaz looked at Sherry in shock, then turned to Ellison.

He jumped up and grabbed a frisbee. "Who wants to play?" With a giggle Sherry and two other girls ran after him. Jaz grabbed her water bottle and backpack and walked away in the opposite direction. Nobody even asked why she was leaving.

That night, her mom dropped a bombshell that forced Jaz to take action. "Do not plan anything with your friends this Saturday. I am going to take you shopping for things for your dorm room."

From the little Jaz heard about her mom's parents she knew that they never learned English. They put her in regular kindergarten only able to speak Chinese. The experience was traumatic for her.

Although she never completely lost her accent, she always spoke carefully. Other people thought it was because English was her second language. Jaz knew it was because she insisted on perfection and following the rules in everything she did.

"Oh, uh, I was thinking of just using the stuff from my room. It's fine Mommy, I don't need anything else."

"Do not be silly. Of course you do. And we should order you a proper winter coat and boots, plus new fall and winter clothes. It will be much colder there."

"No, really, it's OK Mommy. Please. I don't need anything else."

At that moment her dad walked in from work. "Stanley, talk some sense into this girl. She thinks she does not need to go shopping for university!"

He sighed, putting down his briefcase on the floor before sinking into one of the matching white Sloan wingback chairs in the living room. "I'm sure she didn't mean it Allison. Of course she'll go shopping with you."

She turned to Jaz and glared. "Jasmine? Have you changed your mind?"

Jaz looked from her mom to her dad. She had spent her entire life doing what they expected of her. And she knew they had spent their entire lives doing what was expected of them. It was a long cycle of everyone doing the right thing and never making stupid mistakes. Until now.

"Mommy, Daddy?" she took a big breath. It was time to tell them. She couldn't hide her pregnancy forever. Just as she was about to continue, her mom's phone rang. Going into the dining room she took the call while Jaz stood there awkwardly, looking at the floor. In turn, her dad stared at his hands.

"That was the Lawson's. They have invited us to meet them for cocktails and then go to the symphony. It is last minute so you will have to change right away Stanley." She turned to Jaz, "I am not done with you. We will talk tomorrow."

And with that, Jaz lost the nerve to say anything. She watched her parents hustle out the door ten minutes later, eager to please their important friends. Her dad looked back once as they left, as if he wanted to say something, but he never did. The comfort she desperately wanted from her parents left the house when they did. And then she curled up on the couch while tears streamed down her face and pooled on the grey cashmere blanket that was carefully draped over the corner.

The next morning Jaz's morning sickness forced her to dash to the bathroom before her mom left for her run.

"Jasmine? Why are you throwing up? Did you get drunk last night?"

"No Mommy," she moaned. Her parents didn't even have alcohol in the house. How could she have gotten drunk?

"I am not leaving until you come out here and tell me what is going on… Stanley? Come down here!"

Jaz rested her forehead on the edge of the toilet bowl. It was too much to keep it all in. She needed her parents right now. She slowly stood up and splashed some cold water on her face before drying her hands and face and opening the door. Both parents stood there—a rare event in the morning.

"What is going on Jasmine?" Her mother stood there in her running gear. Although she was only an inch taller than Jaz, she seemed to loom over her. With her hands on her hips and her shoulders thrown back she was completely intimidating.

"I… I'm pregnant." As soon as she said the words, she wished she could crawl into the ground and never come out. Her dad looked heartbroken. But her mom's look said everything. She was furious.

"WHAT? Are you sure?"

"Yeah. I, um, I saw a doctor—"

"—How *dare* you do this to us? After everything we have done for you, this is how you thank us? Do you even know who the father is?" She held up her hand to stop Jaz from answering, "How could you? I told you all those white boys will just use you."

"No, mommy, it wasn't like—"

"—Do not talk to me. Get your things and get out. You have ruined my life. When I get back from my run I expect you to be gone."

"Mommy, no!" Jaz reached out her hands to her mom, but she spun on her heel and marched away. Seconds later she heard the front door slam.

"Daddy, it's not like that! Please!"

In those few seconds Jaz felt like her dad aged ten years. His face paled, his shoulders dropped, and he bowed his head as he walked away from her.

Stunned, Jaz walked to her room. With shaking hands she pulled on a pair of white shorts and a navy blue short-sleeve button up shirt. She grabbed her phone and charger and put them in her backpack along with her laptop, some changes of clothes and a framed picture of her with her grandma when she was five years old. It crossed her mind that she should grab her grandma's sewing machine from the garage because she needed the comfort of her right now, but she didn't think she could carry it. Grabbing her purse, she put her backpack over one shoulder and walked out the door.

She doesn't really mean it. She just needs some time. Jaz walked down the street and sat at the bus stop bench. Twenty minutes later her mom ran past on her way back home. If she saw her daughter sitting there, she didn't let on. Shortly after, her dad and then her mom drove by on their way to work. After waiting a few more minutes Jaz got up and walked home. She tried her code for the front door five times before it dawned on her that her parents had really, truly kicked her out.

She turned away from her home and slowly walked down the road. At the park where she had pretended to be a normal teenager just a few days earlier she sat on a bench and tried to make sense of things. Her parent's response was completely unexpected. She knew they'd be upset, but it had never crossed her mind that they might kick her out. Taking out her phone she texted her mom:

I'm so sorry.

Then she used her banking app to check her balance. She never worried about money—her parents deposited $200 in her account every month for spending money. If there was ever anything she wanted that was more than that, she just asked for it. Hiding away from everyone for the past month and a half had at least cut her spending. She had $386.27 in her account. If she needed, that could pay for a hotel. But then what? She hadn't been able to get a job. In fact, she hadn't even been called for a single interview. All the student jobs in the city were taken by now.

Tears began to spill out of her eyes. It wasn't fair. She made one mistake. One. But so had Ellison. And he wasn't suffering at all! Of course, he did say he could help her with money. She debated asking him for help. He'd probably call her stupid again at the very least. Jaz wasn't used to being looked down on. She had spent her entire life being the good girl, blending in with the friends her mom approved of, and doing what she was told. Now there was nobody to tell her what to do.

At some point she started to feel hungry. Getting up, she made her way through the park and back into the city. A little café she had never been in caught her eye and she went in to try and eat. She made her order of toast last as long as she could, but eventually she had no more reason to stay there.

After paying she continued to wander aimlessly through the streets, avoiding all the places she thought her friends might hang out. She was tired, but felt like she needed to keep walking until she figured something out. When she found herself in front of the clinic where she got her pregnancy test, she decided to just sit inside for a while to give her legs a rest. She sat in a chair in the corner and tucked her legs up underneath her.

CHAPTER 4

"*H*ey, Jaz? Jaz?"

Jaz slowly opened her eyes. Someone had her hand on her shoulder and was gently shaking her. She looked up into the kind eyes of the lady who had seen her at the clinic weeks ago.

"Ah, there you are. Hey hon, we're closing up here. Did you want to see me?"

"Oh, um... no." She tried to remember the lady's name but couldn't. Her body ached from being curled up in the chair. Looking at the phone clenched in her hand she could see that it was 4:30. And her mom hadn't texted back. The only notifications were streams of group chats about hanging out.

"OK, well we need to close up here. This is our early closing day."

Jaz followed the lady out of the clinic and watched her walk to a minivan parked at the end of the parking lot. Looking around, she tried to remember what was nearby. It wasn't a neighborhood she was familiar with. All she wanted was a safe place for the night.

"Jaz?"

She looked up to see the lady in her van with the window rolled down. Slowly she walked past other parked cars to the open window.

"Hon, do you have anywhere to go?"

Jaz looked down, feeling the shame of the day pour over her. She shook her head, not bothering to stop the tears that quickly dripped onto the pavement.

"I can take you somewhere safe, OK?"

Without raising her head she nodded. She didn't even care where it was, she just wanted the day to be over.

"You're gonna need to get in. When you're ready. I'll wait."

Jaz looked up through the tears and made her way around to the passenger side. Her mind flashed to a time when she was twelve and had gone with a friend and her noisy family for a day at an amusement park. It was the first and only time she rode in a minivan and was still one of her happiest memories. The family moved a few months later.

"Just ignore the mess. I'm the proud mom of three boys which means my life and my van are kind of a disaster. But at least it's never boring! I'm Kara by the way, it's been a while since we've chatted." She pulled out her phone from her purse and typed something in. A minute later she smiled and put the phone back before turning to Jaz.

"What happened?"

"I, um... My parents. My mom. I told her this morning. She said I had to leave. They changed the code on the locks. I tried to text her..." Jaz wiped away the tears that kept falling. She never used to cry, but now it felt like she couldn't stop crying.

"Oh wow, that's rough. I'm taking you to my friend Carrie's. She's got a cute little house, and two kids that you're going to fall in love with." She turned to smile at Jaz before putting the van in drive.

"They're *way* calmer than my older boys! Anyways, Carrie's amazing. Before we get there is there anything you need? Did you have a chance to pack some things before you left?"

"I'm OK." she whispered in answer.

Jaz kept her backpack clutched to her stomach when the van stopped. "Do you have any money?" Kara asked.

"Yeah, I've got money in a bank account." She got out after Kara and followed her up a path to a little house. There was barely time for the doorbell to ring before a woman opened it.

"Hello! Come on in!"

Following Kara's lead, Jaz slipped off her runners and followed her to a table, still hanging on to her backpack.

"Coffee or tea?"

"Definitely coffee for me!" Kara sat down at the table, and the other lady—Carrie?—walked over to the kitchen and turned her coffee maker on.

Jaz kept her head down. When a mug was placed in front of her, she looked up to see a cup of hot chocolate. The lady giving it to her had a messy ponytail of brown wavy hair, soft brown eyes, and a gentle smile. She sat down at an angle to Jaz as Jaz looked down into her lap again.

"Carrie, this is Jaz. Jaz, my good friend Carrie.... Jaz is about three months pregnant. She just told her parents today and they insisted she leave."

Feeling tears threaten to begin falling again, Jaz tried to clench her jaw. A hand came into her view and gently rested on her arm.

"I'm so sorry," she heard Carrie say. "I know you don't know me at all, but I've been through some tough stuff and survived. I'm happy to be here for you, if you'll let me."

The kindness was too much, and again tears started to fall. It made

Jaz wish desperately that it was her own mom reaching out to her, and not some stranger.

"Would you like to stay here for a little while? I have to warn you, I have a quiet eleven-year-old son and a very loud, but very cute six-year-old daughter. She'll probably decide you're her new best friend. You'd have to share a bathroom with the rest of us because this house only has one bathroom, but we could give you a bit of privacy downstairs."

Jaz couldn't believe it. What kind of person just offered a teenager a place to stay? She wished she had a plan that didn't involve other people, but right now she couldn't think of anything else to do.

"Yes please," she whispered.

Carrie and Kara started to talk, and then Kara turned to Jaz, "I'm sorry. It seems like I'm talking as if you're not here. I think I'm just trying to save you from having to talk. Is that OK? I'm not offended easily so say whatever you want."

"No, please talk."

"Alright." She turned back to Carrie, "Well, medically speaking the best thing for Jaz right now is to be in a safe place without stress where she can work out what she wants to do next. She has her own bank account with some money in it."

"You keep that money for yourself. I want you to have some time here with as little stress as possible. OK?"

Jaz nodded.

Kara stood up, "I have to get going. But I'm happy to leave you two to get to know each other. And Jaz, you have my cell number. Text me whenever OK?"

Again Jaz nodded, and when Kara got up to leave she waited at the table, unsure of what to do next.

After seeing Kara out, Carrie sat down beside her, "The kids are playing at the playground around the corner but they'll be back soon. You don't have to talk if you don't want to, but is there anything you want me to know before they come back?"

Jaz finally made eye contact before dropping her gaze again. "I'm sorry." She felt terrible about bringing her problems into someone else's house. Her mom would be mortified to hear that she was imposing on a stranger. It had been drilled into her from an early age that they never let problems leave their own front door. And now she was just throwing herself at random women she didn't even know.

"Hon, you're not in trouble with me, and you definitely haven't done anything wrong to me. And I hope you'll see one day that this is not the end for you. It might be a different story than you thought you'd have, but different will be ok." Carrie brought over a box of Kleenex and Jaz grabbed a few. Suddenly the sound of kids came in through the open window that faced the backyard. She tried to dry her eyes and pretend to be fine.

A voice started chatting excitedly the second the back door opened, "Hi Mommy! We're back! Uncle Jonathan was there with Angela and he pushed us both really high on the — *Who* are *you?*"

Jaz looked up to see the cutest girl standing in front of her with her hands on her hips. She was wearing pink shorts and a pink t-shirt and her brown curly hair was held back with two pink hair clips. She was a perfect tiny copy of Carrie. Behind her was a boy who Jaz thought was maybe nine or ten. He looked from Jaz to Carrie and back to Jaz.

She felt herself smiling at the little girl — she couldn't help it. "I'm Jaz. Who are you?"

"I'm Katie. And this is Matthew. And this is our house. But you can stay here. That's a funny name."

"It's short for Jasmine. But I prefer Jaz."

Katie's eyes got wide, "Like Princess Jasmine! And you have the skin like hers! Are you a princess?"

"Nope, definitely not a princess." She couldn't be further from a Disney princess. Jaz sat and looked at everyone as Katie went into the kitchen and struggled to pour four glasses of lemonade. She couldn't believe Carrie just sat there and let her do it. When Katie triumphantly put a half-full glass in front of Jaz, she smiled again. It occurred to her that she had just smiled twice in less than ten minutes. A short while ago she wouldn't have believed she was even capable of smiling again.

"Matthew, can you show Jaz around the house? We'll give her a space of her own in the basement, but she needs to know where the bathroom is. And Katie? Your turn to set the table while I start supper." Carrie got up and went into the kitchen.

Jaz turned to Matthew, "Come on this way," he said gently. Jaz followed him down the stairs into a cozy looking basement. There was a faded couch, some beanbag chairs, a TV and a table with chairs.

"This is where you'll sleep. It's nice and cool in the summer. Did you want to put your backpack down?"

"Oh, yeah, sure." Jaz debated keeping her phone with her but decided to leave it. She didn't even need it if she had no one to text.

She followed Matthew back upstairs and through the main floor to the upstairs where he showed her the bathroom and their bedrooms. It was the smallest house Jaz had ever been in, but there was a feeling about the place that she liked. Coming back downstairs she let herself look around. The front door opened into the living room area where there was a bright orange couch and an armchair covered in a colorful fabric.

On the walls were an assortment of colorful empty frames that somehow looked really cool, and there was a bright blue coffee table that held a Nintendo Switch controller, and a coloring book and crayons. A doll was propped up on an armchair with a bright tropical print.

20

"Make yourself at home," Carrie called from the kitchen. "Supper will just be another fifteen minutes."

Unsure what to do, Jaz sat on the edge of the couch. "Oh wow." She scooted back further and felt like the couch was hugging her.

Matthew smiled and sat down beside her, "Everyone does that. It's like the world's most comfortable couch. My mom got it at a yard sale. She finds lots of good deals." He picked up the controller and started playing.

Jaz continued to look around. Through the big front window she could see a tidy front yard, and other small houses around. It was almost a different world from her own where big showy houses were placed to overpower each other. To her left, there was a wall between the living room and kitchen, but the entire area was fairly open — though tiny compared to the cavernous spaces in her parent's house.

Katie suddenly came over, grabbed the doll and sat right next to Jaz. "This is Mirabella. She's my favorite dolly. I have another one upstairs. And I have teddy bears too. Do you have a daddy?"

Her question shocked Jaz, "Um, yeah."

"I do, but he's gone at jail. He's not very nice."

"Katie," Matthew interrupted.

Her face fell for a moment, and then she seemed to recover. "What grade are you in? I'm all done kindergarten now. In grade one I'll have a new teacher. Her name is Mrs. M."

She continued to chat until Carrie called them to the table. "I hope you're OK with spaghetti and meat sauce." Jaz sat down where Katie directed her, and surprised herself by eating a full serving. A whole day of not eating very much had caught up to her. For someone used to quiet suppers with just her mom, she was amazed at the amount of conversation the other three had while they ate.

It was Matthew's job to clean up afterwards, and she offered to help. But it was pretty obvious he was much more experienced than she was. After moving the plastic cups she had just put in the dishwasher from the bottom rack to the top, he deadpanned, "You need way more practice."

Shocked, she stopped and stood staring at him until he let a smirk catch the corners of his mouth. She laughed out loud, "Nice try. Maybe I'll just sit and watch instead," she teased back.

Their banter continued until everything was cleaned up. Then Carrie came back in and started setting painting supplies up on the table.

"I have a business refinishing and repurposing frames," she explained as she laid things out on the table. "During the summer I work on projects in the morning and then leave everything to dry for the afternoon while the kids and I entertain ourselves."

"That's so cool! Do you have a shop or something?"

"Nope, everything's sold online. I started off using a buy and sell site, but now I have my own website where I list everything. It's almost all shipped out from the house. And a friend of mine is an artist, so she brings her completed pieces here and I take care of listing them and shipping them out. You'll meet her tomorrow morning, and her gorgeous daughter Brittany."

"Yay!" Katie called from the coffee table where she was coloring, "Brittany's coming!"

Jaz was dying to ask her all about her business and how she made money. She had never met someone who made a living as an artist. But she was too shy to speak up. Instead, she watched Carrie for a few minutes before walking over to the wall with the eclectic mix of frames. Just looking at all the colors made her feel happier—and like she was in a different universe. The living room at her parent's home was a very carefully arranged white and grey designer showcase. Even the art was black and white photos in silver frames. This living room with its mishmash of colors and styles couldn't be more different, and yet somehow Jaz felt comfortable here.

CHAPTER 5

The next morning Jaz barely got upstairs to the bathroom before being sick. She had slept well on the mattress Carrie set up for her, but as soon as she was awake the morning sickness kicked in. She hoped that the bathroom fan would hide the sound of her being sick. When she left the bathroom, both of the kid's doors were still closed and she sighed in relief.

In the kitchen, Carrie was just making a cup of coffee. "Hey there," she smiled through half-open eyes, "I'd say good morning but it sounds like maybe mornings aren't your best time. Do you want to try some weak tea? It helped me with my morning sickness."

"Um, yeah. OK." Jaz sat at the table where Carrie had already pushed aside the plastic covering enough to set up her laptop. As she sipped her tea she was surprised that it did help a bit—or at least didn't make things worse. Pretty soon she was watching as Carrie show her the *Framed* business website and everything on it.

"I keep all the finished product in the furnace room downstairs. Right now I'm trying to stock up so that I can keep sales going when I start school again in September. I'm finishing my master's degree and it's sooooo much work. But the business is covering all my expenses so I can't complain."

"Where else do you have a presence?"

Carrie looked at her blankly, "A presence?"

"Yeah, you know, an online presence. Instagram, Facebook, Pinterest.... Wait. You're making all these sales without social media?"

"I guess so. It's lots of word of mouth, and one of my friends who does online consulting has some frames up in her office where her clients can see them, so I've gotten some good sales with that."

"You totally need to branch out! I can help you, I'm always on Instagram!" Immediately Jaz regretted opening her mouth. What right did she have to tell Carrie what to do? And Instagram was a silly waste of time. She was lucky her mom hadn't blocked her from using it.

"Oh really? I'm more of a Pinterest girl myself, but I never thought of it for the business. What's your favorite stuff on Instagram?"

Jaz looked down and felt embarrassed. She knew all her friends followed the usual list of influencers. And she pretended to as well, but her entire feed was fashion designers. "So, it's kinda all fashion designers." When Carrie simply looked interested, Jaz warmed up, "There's all these really cool designers on there. I can look at clothes all day!"

"Huh. I never even knew about that. I thought Instagram was just for rich people putting up pictures of their fancy life all day."

Jaz giggled, "Well, there's that, but there's way more, too. I could start you an account for your business, and teach you how to use it if you want."

"That's so sweet, but I'm not capable of learning anything new right now. There's only so much new information I can fit in my brain right now!"

"I can do it for you." She hoped she hadn't gone too far. Her mom always told her she needed to speak less and listen more.

Carrie looked at her for a moment, struggling between the need for help and her hesitance in putting any pressure on this vulnerable teenager. "You know, I'd really appreciate that. But any time it gets too much, you just tell me. No pressure, OK?"

At that point Matthew wandered down the stairs, and Carrie walked over to meet him at the couch. She kissed his forehead, and then sat down and he cuddled into her. Jaz felt like it was a mother-son moment that was private, but she couldn't look away. There was something so safe about their relationship with each other.

For the first time, she wondered what it would be like to be a mom. Her own mom would sometimes relax enough for them to enjoy being together, but it didn't happen often. Most of the time her mom was checking on everything Jaz was supposed to be doing—school, volunteering, university applications, keeping her room perfect. Jaz wondered if they'd have anything to talk about now that she wasn't going to university. If her mom ever talked to her again.

She went downstairs and started tidying up her bedding. It looked like the kids used this room as a play area and she didn't want to be in the way. Reaching over to unplug her cell phone, she saw a chat that had come in during the night. Normally she ignored them unless everyone was planning to do something, but seeing her own name caught her attention.

Hey, what the heck's up with Jaz? Why didn't she tell us?

What do you mean?

She left for a gap year! Her mom told Ellison's mom yesterday. Said she wouldn't be back til next summer. And she's 'taking a break' from everything so we can't even follow her!

What a bitch. She always acted like she was so much better than us.

God, she couldn't even tell us she wasn't going to university this fall? I'm so done with her.

Me too. Obvs 'miss perfect' doesn't need us now that school's out.

The thread continued, but Jaz couldn't read any more. These were the people she considered her friends. And not one of them tried to reach out and see if the rumor was true. They just assumed the worst. Well, at least none of them guessed she was pregnant. But she was shocked to see what they actually thought of her. She deleted the app and then sat there for a while, trying to figure out what to do next.

"Princess Jasmine?" The little voice at the top of the stairs interrupted Jaz's thoughts.

"Yeah Katie?"

"Can I come down?"

"Of course!"

"Yay!" with far too much energy Katie bounced down the stairs in her Disney princess pajamas. "Look! It's you!" she claimed, pointing to Princess Jasmine.

"You know I'm not a princess, right?"

"Yes you are!" Katie sat down practically on top of Jaz and cuddled into her. Awkwardly Jaz was forced to wrap one arm around her. "I like you Princess Jasmine. I'm glad you're staying with us."

Jaz felt a little smile tug at the corner of her mouth. After reading the cruel comments about her, all it took was a six-year-old's innocent statement to make her feel better. She wondered how long Katie would stay there. Seconds later her question was answered when Katie bounced up.

"What do you want to do today? We can go to the park with Matthew this morning while Mommy works. And maybe she'll take us to the lake—I like it there! And we should collect more pop cans because I want more candy, and—"

She was interrupted by Carrie. "—Katie, come on upstairs. That's Jaz's space now."

Jaz followed her upstairs.

"But Mommy, I asked before I went down, and Princess Jasmine said yes!"

"Excellent! I'm glad you asked first. But we still need to respect Jaz's space."

"It's OK, she can come down whenever she wants."

Carrie smiled, "Well, now you've basically begged me for the boundaries lecture!" she looked at Jaz's confused face before continuing, "All of us have the right to boundaries. That means honoring ourselves enough to not let people run all over us, and saying 'No' when something's not right for you."

She grabbed Katie from behind and gave her a cuddle as she continued, "Even if this little package of sweetness wants something, it's important for you to say 'No' if you don't want it. And that should maybe include you making sure you have some space to be alone when you need it."

Jaz wasn't sure what to say. Carrie and Katie didn't look upset at all, so she didn't think she needed to apologize. But she didn't feel she had a right to say no to Katie, either. It went against everything she had been taught her entire life.

"So, you're maybe thinking that sounds selfish and wrong, right?" Carrie seemed to see right through Jaz.

"Yeah, how did you know?"

"It's the difference between being raised in an individualistic society like the one I know, and the collective society like the one I'm guessing you know—where you're expected to do what's right for your community or family, not yourself personally."

Jaz felt her mouth drop open. Was that racist? She didn't think so...

"Personally, I think there's value in both approaches. We do need to think about the impact of our choices on others. But we also need to give ourselves the utmost respect and consideration." She looked down on Katie, "Because whose job is it to take care of you?"

Katie giggled, "Yours?"

"Try again silly girl!"

Katie looked at Jaz, "It's my job to take care of me and your job to take care of you!" She danced away singing the phrase to some nonsense tune.

CHAPTER 6

*J*az spent the morning setting up accounts for Carrie's business on Instagram and Facebook. It was fun to add in all the amazing frames and art. The whole trend with upcycling was really taking off, and with a few carefully chosen hashtags Jaz was pretty sure the accounts would get more followers soon.

She even learned how to set up items to sell right from Instagram—you could learn anything with a few YouTube videos—but Carrie said she didn't want to include another place for sales just yet. Jaz was amazed at how Carrie could say 'no thanks' so easily, and then just move on with her day. She didn't seem at all worried about how other people might feel—she wasn't worried about offending people or doing something that would upset them—and yet everything she did came across as kind and caring.

When Lauren came over with Brittany, Jaz was confused all over again. Lauren looked rough. Her faded jean shorts showed pure white bony legs, her t-shirt had a DIY fringe along the shoulders that Jaz was pretty sure went out of style in the 80s, and her blonde hair hung straight down on either side of her face. She was friendly to Jaz when Carrie introduced them, but Jaz found herself trying to figure out how someone like Lauren was friends with someone like Carrie.

"Hey Matthew, grab the kid for me so I can get my stuff!"

Happily Matthew came over and helped Brittany take off her sandals before carrying her over to the living room and carefully sitting her down on the floor. She was the opposite of her mom, wearing an adorable yellow romper with her thin blonde hair up in two ponytails. Matthew pulled a basket of toys out from under the coffee table, and sat beside her. Katie sat on her other side and dumped the toys out.

When Lauren came back in with her arms full of paintings, Jaz could only stare. She already had an idea of what Lauren could do after putting up images that morning, but seeing them in real life was something else. The paintings were all different sizes and styles, but each one seemed to have something about it that made you want to get a closer look.

Lauren and Carrie started talking about the paintings and what to charge for them. Carrie made little post-its with the title and price to stick on the back of each one, and then they went over to the table and chatted about the frames Carrie had put out the night before.

Jaz tried to stay out of the way, but she couldn't help listening to everything they were saying. In the world she grew up in, 'business' was all about suits, meetings, and trying to please a boss that was always demanding more. What these two women were doing was obviously successful, but didn't fit with what Jaz thought running a business meant. And the weird thing was that they both looked so happy.

"Pardon me?" She realized Lauren had been talking to her.

"You got something to say. So spit it out."

"I just, um, I don't understand how this works. How you make it work." She vaguely waved her hand across the table and Lauren's paintings stacked neatly beside the door to the laundry room.

"You've got this Lauren, I'll make coffee." Carrie went into the kitchen, and Lauren gestured to Jaz to sit down.

"Last year I was knocked up, and like, just done with everything. My boyfriend was blowin' all his money on drugs and we were in a shelter. Then this broad shows up," she waved in Carrie's direction, "the day after we get a place and she's like, all nice to us and sh… stuff. I mean, she comes by to see if there's mail 'cause she used to live there, and then 'bam she's all, like, helpful, and brings a baby gift, and has me over for coffee."

Carrie came to the table with coffees, and another tea for Jaz. She sat down, and raised her hand, "I'd be the broad, in case you were wondering." She didn't seem offended at all by Lauren's comment, and nearly swearing in front of the kids.

"So yeah," Lauren continued, "I had the baby, and then she says said she'll pay me to paint frames—and I *really* needed money. And then my boyfriend OD'd and nearly died. And then I had this idea to take shitty paintings from the thrift stores and make them better. And then Carrie started selling them. And now I make a crap-load of money. All because of her." She raised her mug in a silent toast to Carrie, who smiled and raised hers in return.

"This whole business is about seeing opportunities. I started out two years ago taking things out of dumpsters and fixing them up to sell them." Carrie didn't seem to notice Jaz's horrified face. "It grew from there into a business that can support two families. I feel like there's chances all around us to make things better and earn a living, we just have to see them."

"And if Miss Sunshine here don't float your boat, then see it my way. I get paid to paint. Best thing ever."

Jaz had so many questions. About Carrie, Lauren, the business, Lauren's druggie boyfriend. But she didn't want to upset them by asking. So she watched quietly as they talked and planned next steps for the business. When they finished, Lauren checked her watch and got up to leave.

"Dustin's physio's done now so we should go."

"Is this therapist going to last?"

Lauren snorted, "She's another little pansy, but maybe tougher than the last one. I warned her about the swearing before she started though."

"Aw, look at you getting all soft in your old age!" Carrie teased.

Lauren rolled her eyes, "I'm just tired of breaking new ones in." She looked over at Jaz, "Dustin can't talk in sentences, but try to make him do exercises and he turns the air blue with swears. We're trying not to let Brittany hear so I always come here when he has physio."

"Oh, right." She had no idea what they were talking about. After they left, Carrie got to work on her frames and the kids went to the park. Jaz decided to work on the social media accounts. It was the least she could do for Carrie.

As if she realized Jaz's confusion about Lauren, Carrie talked while she sanded the frames on the table. "Dustin overdosed last December. It was touch and go for days, but he did survive, obviously. But the brain damage was pretty bad. He's partially paralyzed on one side of his body and has trouble talking. The physio Lauren was talking about is something they're just getting into now that they can afford it. I hope it helps. Dustin's such a great guy!"

"But he's an addict."

"Yeah, he is. And he'll probably always struggle with that. But he's also a nice guy who loves his little family. It's amazing how he's figured out how to take care of Brittany with his disabilities. And it's the only way Lauren could do so much painting. You'll see what a great guy he is when you meet him."

They were quiet for a while, both working on their projects. Jaz's image of a drug addict was a guy slumped in an alley with a needle hanging out of his arm. She couldn't understand how an addict could be a family guy, or even a good person for that matter.

After eating a lunch of grilled cheese sandwiches at the backyard picnic table, Carrie and the kids decided to go to the lake. She invited Jaz to join them. "Even if you don't swim, it's nice to relax and dig your toes into the sand."

Jaz desperately wanted to say yes, but the chance of running into kids from school was too risky. "I, um, I think I should stay here and rest."

"Are you sick Princess Jasmine?" Katie looked distressed at the thought of her new friend not feeling well.

Carrie saved her from answering, "Jaz has had a really busy past couple of months, and now she needs to rest lots and take care of herself."

"OK! If you rest enough you can play with me tonight, OK?" Again she cuddled right up to Jaz, and the contact felt surprisingly nice.

"Yeah, sure."

After they left, Jaz went downstairs and lay on the carpet. It felt safer on the floor. Maybe because she felt like she could hide away from everything there. She pulled out her phone and clicked on Instagram. Soon, the images of all the unique, colorful outfits that were such a contrast to her own perfectly organized life distracted her enough that she could doze off.

A notification startled her awake. Thinking it was her mom she quickly grabbed at her phone. But it was just an email from the school, confirming her final grades. Straight A's and a GPA of 4.0. On paper she was perfect. In real life? A total failure. She wandered upstairs, wondering when Carrie and the kids would get back. If only there was something she could do for them, but she didn't know how to cook, or clean, or any of the other things someone like Carrie needed help with.

Jaz wondered about her. How did she become single? The comment from Katie about her dad being in jail was weird. Carrie didn't seem like the type to marry a criminal. Actually, she seemed like the type to marry a super nice guy and have a happy normal life. She was definitely a good mom though.

For the second time, Jaz thought about being a mom. Would she be any good at it? Or would it even be fair to her baby? If Ellison was right, and nobody would want to adopt an Asian baby, what would happen? Foster care? Jaz thought that was pretty bad, but maybe not as bad as having a teen mom.

It felt like she had been transported to a different world. She had never in her life thought about being pregnant—even when she got older. Never. And even though there was no way to deny it now, or pretend it wasn't going to happen, it still felt like it couldn't possibly be real. For her entire life she had been told her role in life was to go to med school, graduate at the top of her class, and become a respected surgeon.

Having a baby and being a single mom was so far away from the life plan she was expecting that she felt lost, confused, and scared. If her life could take this big of a shift because of one night, what else could change?

It was better when the house was full of the constant chatter of Katie again. It gave her a break from her own worries. That night 'Uncle Jonathan' came over, bringing all the fixings for ice cream sundaes, and staying to play games. Jaz had heard Katie talking about him, but was shocked when a tall, surfer-type guy showed up at the door. He was much younger than Jaz had pictured. She had an uncle of her own who came over once for a visit, but he was as old as her dad.

It took about a minute for Jaz to see that there was some serious chemistry between Jonathan and Carrie, and they both seemed to pretend there wasn't. Despite her own disastrous hook-up, Jaz found herself rooting for them to become a couple.

Matthew and Katie seemed oblivious to the connection between their mom and Jonathan, but they clearly thought the world of him. Jaz watched all the interactions carefully. They were all so different from her own family. Katie was always hugging everyone—something Jaz didn't think she had ever done as a child—and Carrie and Jonathan were constantly engaging the kids in conversations, and complimenting them, too. It was such a contrast to her own upbringing where she was expected to stay in the background, and was rarely acknowledged by other adults.

While Carrie seemed perfectly happy letting the kids make their own extravagant ice cream creations, she also insisted they help clean up afterwards. And the kids didn't really seem to mind. Then they all played Candyland together. Apparently it was Katie's favorite game, and she was happy to teach Jaz how to play. After Katie went to bed, Jonathan and Matthew continued a game they had going on the Nintendo Switch, and Carrie sat and read a book.

Jaz joined them on the couch and surfed on her phone, but still paid close attention to the interactions going on around her. She didn't understand why Carrie and Jonathan weren't together, but she was far too embarrassed to even think of asking Carrie about it. She'd just have to keep on watching them, but if she had a chance, she'd do her best to help them get together.

CHAPTER 7

Over the next few days Jaz encouraged Carrie to get her friends involved in sharing the different social media accounts. That, along with some of the hashtags she was using seemed to grow a following pretty quickly. Carrie even gave her the login to her website (something that shocked Jaz, and made her feel pretty good), and she could see that referrals from Instagram and Facebook were definitely contributing to more traffic.

When Carrie jokingly suggested that Jaz needed to help her with frames because she had created too much new business, she jumped at the chance to help. Carrie claimed that there was no way she could mess up the frames. Anything that didn't look quite right could be fixed. Jaz was terribly nervous at first, always trying to make things look perfect even when the paint was still wet. But Carrie continued to insist that decent was the goal—not perfect, and Jaz began to feel more confident. She loved how it felt to turn something boring—and usually brown—into something bright and colorful.

Many of the frames were sold as empty frames, meant to stand on their own or in a group. As Jaz went through old listings to get a better feel for the products, she was amazed at the variety Carrie could come up with. For starters, everything she used came from either the thrift store or yard sales. Jaz had never been to either and was under the impression they were full of cheap crap. Apparently not!

While many of the empty frames were various bright colors, others were mismatched sets all with the same finish. Jaz loved the black frames with gold accents that looked antique. And other frames were filled with squares of vintage fabric that Carrie also found used. How she could turn an old hippie skirt into a framed piece of art was beyond Jaz's comprehension. But being able to be a part of such a cool business was fun, and made her feel slightly grown up for the first time ever.

Every afternoon when Carrie and the kids went out they'd invite Jaz along, but she declined. She was still afraid of running into her friends, while at the same time the feeling of security she got at Carrie's place made her want to stay there forever. Even when the kids fought, or Carrie disciplined one of them, there was always this feeling in the house that made Jaz feel good.

In the afternoons Jaz would post things for the business, and she started reading pregnancy sites. Her mom had never talked about her pregnancy or delivery, and she hadn't been around anyone pregnant before. It felt like she had a lot to learn.

Kara stopped by one evening with her youngest son Magnus to see how she was doing. At first Jaz thought she was just visiting Carrie, but after an hour she clued in that Kara really was making sure she was OK. It made her want to cry that a stranger cared enough about her to come and see her. But at least she wasn't crying all the time anymore. And Kara brought prenatal vitamins for her, saying she had some free packages from work.

In high school it had been easy to fit in. She had the right clothes, the right friends, she did the right sports, and she got the right grades. But now that all of that was gone, Jaz was realizing it had never been about *her*. It had been about appearances. And now here was Carrie; someone who didn't dress well or have an important job but she was happy. Jaz smirked. Maybe this 34-year-old was the first real friend she had.

Between being surrounded by people who accepted her, and having time to think about her situation, Jaz started to realize that she wanted to keep her baby. She read enough adoption stories online to understand how hard it would be to follow through with that option. There was a part of her that felt like her baby was the only family she had now that her parents had shut her out and she couldn't imagine letting her baby go.

Family hadn't ever been a part of her life, except for her parents and grandma. As far as she knew, her grandparents on her dad's side had come from China just after getting married. Her grandpa passed away when her dad was still in university. Her grandma had been a seamstress and had run a business out of her home until the week before she died. And her mom never talked about her family.

Already the idea of becoming a surgeon gave her a bad taste in her mouth—it wasn't ever what *she* wanted, but she had never allowed herself to consider not doing it until now. There was something very small inside of her that was starting to ask what she really wanted, now that she was starting to realize what she *didn't* want.

As a little girl, Jaz always went to grandma's after school, and her best childhood memories were of sitting beside her while she worked. By the time she was eight she was helping with things like sewing on buttons, and when she was ten she started using the sewing machine for things like pillow covers. She was allowed to use the scraps to make clothes for her Barbies, and her grandma was always teaching her little tricks that she had learned over the years.

When she passed away four years ago, Jaz had been almost comatose with grief. With two parents busy working, 'ma ma' had been the only person who had the time to sit for hours and listen to her. Somehow she understood how hard it was to live with strict Chinese parents, and she always had a kind word for Jaz's mom when she came to pick Jaz up.

Although her parents meant to clear the apartment and throw everything out after her death, Jaz insisted that they keep the sewing machine. It was the last connection she had to the person who always had time for her. Ma ma's hands were always busy but her ears were always listening to Jaz. She didn't say a lot, but she was always there when Jaz needed her.

She wondered what ma ma would say to her now. Maybe she'd tell her off, but Jaz was sure she would still try to support her. She sighed and looked at her phone again. Now that she had deleted the apps her friends all used she didn't get any notifications. If only her mom would send something—anything.

Later on that night she sat scrolling through Instagram while Matthew and Katie watched a DVD beside her. Carrie had gone to Lauren's for something after Jaz and the kids assured her they would be fine.

When the DVD finished, Matthew leaned over and looked at her phone. "How long have you had your own phone?"

Jaz looked up, "Um, a long time I guess. At least for all of high school."

"Is it expensive? I want a phone but Mom said it was a big commitment to have a phone plan because it costs money every month."

"I don't know. My parents pay for it," she paused. At least they hadn't cut off her phone plan yet. And she really had no idea how much one cost.

"Lucky!"

After the kids and Carrie went to bed, Jaz sat at her laptop and looked up phone plans. Fifty dollars a month seemed like a lot of money if she didn't have a job. She wondered what other things she'd have to pay for. Especially with having a baby.

CHAPTER 8

The next morning she forced herself to talk to Carrie about keeping the baby. She hadn't pushed her at all to make a decision, and Jaz wanted to know what Carrie thought.

"I've decided to keep the baby if I can. Do you think I can?"

"Of course you can. It's entirely your choice. Trust me, there are way worse things in life than being a single mom. And I think being a mom is the most amazing thing in the world."

"Not according to my mom. When I told her I was pregnant she said I had destroyed *her* entire life and she'd never forgive me."

"Ouch."

"Yeah. Getting pregnant was definitely not in their plan for me. Actually, it's the first thing I've ever done without their permission. I tried so hard to be the perfect daughter and make them proud. The one time I don't it wrecks everything."

"Do they know the sperm donor?" She laughed when she saw the expression on Jaz's face. "I don't think guys should be called fathers unless they earn it by being there. But that's just me."

Jaz tried not to look shocked at Carrie's blunt words, "They know him, but they don't know he's the... donor. He's actually the son of their best friends. They decided we should study together while they went out to the symphony. That's when it... happened. It was just one time. I don't even know why I did it. He seemed like he really liked me and I thought he'd like me more. When I told him I was pregnant he begged me not to tell his parents. He promised me he'd help out with money if I never told anyone. You're the first person I've told that to."

"OK, it's definitely your choice whether anyone else knows or not. I totally respect that."

Jaz smirked, "My mom thinks it's a white boy. She'll sure be surprised when the baby comes out all Asian. Well, if she ever sees the baby."

"Do you think she'll come around?"

She felt her eyes start to burn and blinked hard to keep the tears away, "Probably not. I'm an only child, and now I've destroyed the honor of my family. I was supposed to start pre-med this fall. My parents wanted me to become a surgeon."

"What do you want?"

"Me? It's not up to me."

"Actually it is. It's completely up to you. I get that your parents expected you to follow their plan. But they're not in your life right now. And even if they were, it's important that you do what's right for you, even if it's not in their plans."

Jaz sighed, "White people are so different from Asians."

"Well, you're stuck with us now. And as my little sister from a different mother I'm officially declaring you part of my family." She came around the table and put her arm around Jaz and gave her a squeeze before making another coffee. "Hey, thanks again for getting those listings up yesterday. You've got a really artistic eye when it comes to setting them up and photographing them!"

Jaz was relieved Carrie had changed the subject. It was still hard to think about not following her parent's plan for her life. "It's so much fun! I haven't been able to do anything creative for a while because my parents made me quit sewing class so I could add another 'real' course to my schedule."

"You sew?"

"I used to. My grandma was a seamstress." She smiled sadly, "I'd go to her house after school when I was younger and she'd teach me all sorts of stuff. I think she would've been happy to know she was getting a great-grandchild. At least I hope so. She passed away four years ago." Suddenly Jaz sat back and covered her mouth. "Oh my gosh. I'm talking your ear off. Sorry!"

"Don't be! It's called a conversation, and it's way nicer when *you're* talking too."

Katie joined them downstairs and crawled into Carrie's lap for a morning cuddle. "See?" she said to Jaz, "Best thing in the world."

She smiled at Katie, and was surprised again at the happy feeling she got from being around Carrie's kids. "Good morning Katie!"

"Good morning Princess Jasmine!"

Jaz rolled her eyes and pretended to be annoyed, but she secretly liked the way they teased each other.

"Hey," Carrie interrupted her thoughts, "The kids have been invited to go swimming with friends this afternoon. After I drop them off do you want to come with me while I go thrift store shopping?"

"Um, yeah. Thanks!" She was surprised that she did want to go out. Maybe knowing there was no chance she'd run into anyone she knew at the thrift store helped.

At the pool, Jaz waited in the car while Carrie took the kids in but she found herself sinking in her seat anyways, hoping nobody would walk past who might recognize her. She needed some way to change so that she didn't feel so recognizable. At the thrift store she planned on finding new clothes so she could ditch the three preppy outfits she had been rotating through for the past week. Besides, the waistbands on the shorts were already getting uncomfortably tight, and one of her button-up shirts was starting to gape at the bust. *That* was a problem Jaz had never had before, and it made her want to giggle to think about.

"What are you smiling about?" Carrie was getting into the car.

"Who me? Oh, nothing." She felt herself blushing, even though Carrie couldn't know what she had just been thinking about.

The first thing she noticed when they went into the thrift store was the smell. It was a weird combination of fabric softener, dust, and old things. Jaz didn't find it offensive, but she didn't really like it, either.

"I'm going to start with looking through the frames and paintings. If you need anything come find me, OK?"

"Yeah, thanks."

Jaz wandered to the first rack and started flipping through the hangers. The clothes were so tightly packed that she had a hard time looking through them so she just pulled at the sleeves to look at the patterns and fabrics. All her hours of scrolling through pictures of unique outfits made it easy to pull out the things that were unique. She couldn't believe how many cool things were here, and how cheap they were! It would be easy to adjust them to fit, and maybe even make some outfits that would work as she got bigger.

When Carrie found her she already had an armful of clothes. "These are so cool! I can totally change them up to fit me when I start to show." Immediately, reality kicked in. "Oh wait, I forgot I don't have a sewing machine." She turned to start putting things back. The high she had felt from thinking about sewing crashed.

"I do, and you can use it anytime. And what a good idea! I have to tell you, my experience with maternity clothes was that they have way too many bows and ribbons."

Jaz had a flashback to her 2nd grade school picture. Her mom had insisted she wear a blouse with a big bow on the front, and matching bows in two ponytails. Even as a seven-year-old she had known how silly it looked. "Gross. I hate cheesy girly stuff. But with this, I think I can be a hip momma."

"Atta girl!"

The simple compliment from Carrie made Jaz glow. Taking a deep breath, she asked for her first favor from her, "Um, I was wondering. Could you maybe take me to a hair place?"

"Of course! Do you need a trim? Your hair is so gorgeous. I could spend an hour with a flatiron and never be able to make mine look like that!"

"Actually, I was thinking about a big change." Jaz couldn't be honest with her about wanting to look like a different person so her friends wouldn't recognize her.

"There's a hair place just a few doors down. Let's pay for our stuff and load it in the car, and then we can see if they can fit you in. We've still got time. How are you for money?"

"Oh, fine thanks." Jaz hadn't touched her bank account since she had bought lunch the day her parents found out she was pregnant. She took a deep breath.

"You OK?"

She hadn't realized she was standing still. "Um, yeah. I was just— I've wanted to cut my hair short for a long time..."

"And?"

"Well, my parents wouldn't like it." The thought of upsetting them was just as scary as the thought of going ahead and doing what she wanted.

"And?"

Jaz looked up at Carrie, trying to figure out what she wanted her to say. But she didn't look upset or demanding. Actually, she looked like she was genuinely interested in what Jaz had to say.

"Are you sure it's OK to do it?" What she really wanted was for Carrie to tell her what to do.

"What do you think?"

She felt a smile twitch at the corners of her mouth, "You're not going to tell me what to do, are you?"

"Nope!" Now Carrie was smiling too.

She thought back to something Carrie had told Matthew a few days ago, "It's OK to do what you want, as long as you're not taking someone else's rights away." Matthew had wanted to hang out with Jonathan and play guitars, but he felt like he should ask Katie to come. In the end, he had gone to Jonathan's alone, and then come home and played Candyland with Katie later.

"I want to get my hair cut short."

"Great! Let's go see if they can fit you in!"

As the hair fell away, Jaz felt something inside of her shift. This wasn't her disguising herself. This was beginning to show her true self. Between changing her hair and changing her clothes, she was starting to let the 'real' her out. It was scary, but already she was thinking about the little baby growing inside of her. She wanted to raise a child who would feel loved no matter what they accomplished and somehow that included being able to express herself with how she looked.

"Wow." When the stylist turned her chair around after cutting her bangs, Jaz was shocked. Her long, straight hair was gone. In its place was a short bob with micro bangs. It was a look she had gone back to over and over in her Instagram feed, and now she saw the same look framing her own face.

"You've got the perfect hair for this style! Most girls have to work hard to keep it straight and smooth, but you're a natural!"

"Thank you so much!" Jaz turned her face to the left and right, trying to get used to the new woman looking back at her. She just wanted to stay in the chair staring at herself.

When she finally went to pay, she was shocked at the price. "Twenty? That's it?" Her mom had always taken her to a guy down-town who charged five times that for a trim.

"Well, if you really want, feel free to add a tip!" The stylist smiled. She was an older lady, but her own silver hair was in a perfect French twist that suited her. Jaz had been worried she wouldn't know what to do with a modern cut, but she was so happy with the finished product that she added a ten dollar tip.

On her way out, Carrie bumped her shoulder. "You're just like me, I love tipping my hairdresser."

"Actually, that's the first time I've paid for my own haircut. Did I do OK?"

"You did great! And I love your new look!"

It took a few days for Katie to reluctantly accept that Jaz didn't have 'princess hair' anymore, but Carrie complimented Jaz on being such a good role model for Katie. "I want to raise her to just be happy with her own style, whatever it is. But that's easier said than done."

CHAPTER 9

$\mathcal{C}$arrie's old sewing machine took pride of place at the basement table, and Jaz spent many happy hours forgetting about everything else while she altered the clothes to fit her changing body and her new style. She was glad it was in the basement, and she could sew late into the night without worrying about disturbing anyone. And some mornings she even managed to sleep in without starting the day with morning sickness.

She did still struggle with the whole idea of doing what was best for her, without seeing if it was what other people wanted. Often, the time when she and Carrie were working on frames was when they talked things out.

"But it's selfish to focus on what I want. If we all just did what we wanted there would be chaos, and no respect for anyone else."

"Well, yes and no. If we try to get what we want by taking away what is rightfully someone else's then yeah, that would be terrible. *But* if we really listen to what we want deep down inside and we focus on meeting our needs in healthy, respectful ways then the whole world would be a better place."

Jaz bumped her shoulder into Carrie's, "Now who's the Disney Princess with the magical song?"

Laughing, Carrie admitted it did sound too perfect. "But I really think that when we start doing what's best for us we become happier. Too many people go around waiting for someone, or something else to make them happy, when the key is inside of them."

It was obviously easier for Carrie, who had been raised to follow her own goals. Jaz hadn't met her parents yet, but Carrie often talked about how supportive they were.

The next morning when they were all eating breakfast together, Carrie brought up a new 'challenge'. "After breakfast we are going to do something new, and maybe a little weird."

Katie said "Yay!" at the same time as Matthew asked, "Do we have to?"

Jaz didn't dare say anything, but she was definitely on Matthew's side.

Smilling, Carrie answered, "Technically this is all in your head so I can't *make* you. But it's a good thing so I really really hope you do. I read this amazing book last night about loving yourself."

"I love *you* Mommy!"

"Yes, I know you do Katie-girl. But do you love Katie as much as you love Mommy?"

Katie paused, confused. "I don't know."

"See, the thing is we're usually pretty good at loving each other, but maybe not so good at loving ourselves. So sometimes that's why we feel super sad or stressed and we don't know why. It's because we're not loving ourselves."

Jaz disagreed, but again stayed quiet. In comparison to *this* family, her parents hadn't been loving at all! So it wasn't something she thought she was good at.

Wrapping her arms around herself, Katie shook her head, "It's not the same. I want Mommy hugs not Katie hugs."

"You can have all the Mommy hugs you want. And I guess, loving yourself is like giving yourself a mental hug. All you have to do is find a comfy place, play some nice music, close your eyes, and picture God standing by you and giving you lots of loving sunshine around your body while you say, 'I love myself' with every breath."

"And then what happens?" Matthew asked.

Jaz had to force herself not to roll her eyes. If Matthew was getting interested, she'd have to try it too!

"Well, we'd set the timer for five minutes to start. But I tried it this morning in my room, and after five minutes I felt all relaxed, like after I've been in the hot tub. And I really did feel happier too."

"Cool."

"I want us to try doing it every day. But during the day whenever you want you can say 'I love myself' lots. It will help your brain remember how much you're loved! And—" she looked at Jaz, "—it will make everything in your body feel loved too."

Jaz smiled. The kids didn't know about the pregnancy yet, but she knew what Carrie meant. And no matter what, she definitely wanted her baby to feel loved. "Alright alright. I'm in." She pulled out her phone and earbuds. "I'll do it in the basement."

She went downstairs and sat on the floor in the corner. Maybe it was a weird habit she had—to sit on floors or in corners—but it always made her feel safer. It took a minute to find the right music, but she settled on a meditation soundtrack. Pressing play, she put in the earbuds and rested her head against the wall.

What was that Carrie had said? Oh yeah, something about picturing God nearby putting sunshine on you. Jaz didn't really know how to picture God, but she could imagine herself sitting in the sun, getting warm. Slowing her breathing, she started to repeat 'I love myself' just like Carrie had said.

When the sound of feet running around upstairs interrupted her, she was surprised to see that over ten minutes had passed. She sat there for another few minutes before getting up. Something definitely felt different. Like she wasn't worried, and that she really really loved her baby.

When she came upstairs Carrie was setting out some frames, and they worked quietly side by side, each lost in their thoughts. At lunchtime Jaz wanted to keep working, but Carrie could be pretty stubborn when she chose to!

"You've absolutely done enough for today! But if you want to do one more thing, you can log into my shipping account and print off labels for these two packages that need to go out."

Again, Jaz found it amazing that Carrie just let her have access to all her business stuff. But she loved the chance to help send the paintings and frames off. It was nice to know that someone would enjoy something she had a part in making!

After lunch Carrie and the kids went to the nature reserve, and Jaz was happy to go downstairs and do some more sewing. She had been back to the thrift store again with Carrie, this time with more specific things in mind. She still didn't know if she'd be brave enough to wear the things she was creating, but the process made her happier than she had felt in years.

It was weird to think that she could have been getting ready to go to university right now. Although she missed her parents and kept checking her phone to see if her mom would text her back, she was starting to realize that university and being a surgeon had never been her goal in life. She didn't know *what* she wanted besides keeping her baby, but she was starting to figure out what she didn't want.

Being around someone as accepting as Carrie was making it possible for her to start thinking for herself, instead of only trying to please other people. Getting her hair cut was a huge step, but there were other, smaller steps too. Like how it was OK to tease Matthew and pretend to be annoyed when Katie called her Princess Jasmine. And how it was getting easier to hug Katie back during the dozens of times in the day when she'd just come over and hug her, usually while saying something adorable, like "You're the best new big sister ever!"

The things about boundaries that Carrie kept talking to her about were harder to accept, but she desperately wanted to become strong enough to be able to say what she wanted. Slowly she was asking the questions that had always been stifled in the past.

Last week, Lauren asked to come over with Brittany when Carrie and the kids planned to be out. Carrie told Jaz that she didn't have to visit with Lauren if she didn't want to, but when Lauren arrived, Jaz found herself hanging out upstairs.

Sitting on the floor with Brittany she started handing her toys from the basket that Brittany would happily throw away, just to see Jaz get them and give them back to her.

"She can play that game all day!"

Jaz found herself smiling, "I love her belly laugh! Has she always had it?"

"Uh, she started laughing pretty young I guess. It helped Dustin keep trying to get better when he had her around just bein' happy."

"Did you... um... did you *feel* like a mom after she was born?"

"Babe, most of the time I still don't feel like a mom!" Lauren laughed, "I mean, how could I be dealing with that much shit in a day!"

Jaz swiveled her head and looked in shock at Lauren who was sitting on the couch with her feet on the coffee table.

"Diapers Jaz! Shitty diapers!"

"Oh, yeah. Right." Diapers? Jaz had never changed a diaper in her life!

"So, when are you due?"

"Pardon? How do you know?" Her heart started beating faster at the thought that Carrie was talking about her behind her back.

"I may not be the smartest broad, but I figured the only way a chick like you gets kicked out is if you're knocked up or doing drugs. And you ain't the drugs type."

"Oh. OK. Kara thinks the middle of February. I'll know more at my next appointment I think." Relieved that Carrie had kept her secret, *and* that Lauren knew her secret, Jaz found herself wanting to talk about her pregnancy.

"Are you keeping it?"

"Yes." Jaz wrapped her arms around herself, as if to protect her baby. "Definitely."

"And the dad?"

"The *sperm donor*," Jaz smirked, "is too afraid of his parents to own up to anything. He offered me an abortion, and then money, but I said no to both."

"Way to go!" Lauren reached down and offered Jaz a high five. She awkwardly responded. No one had ever high-fived her off the volley-ball court before!

"I was pretty freaked out about being pregnant before Carrie came along." Lauren looked up at her painting on the wall, "She's like a fricken' fairy godmother or something. I dunno what I'd do without her."

"Yeah… she's kinda the first white women I've ever gotten to know. But I think she's pretty awesome."

"Well, don't expect the rest of us white trash to be like her!" Lauren smiled to take the edge of her comment, but Jaz suspected it was a name she had been called a lot before.

"Chink. And ching chong. That's what they call me and my friends. It shouldn't bother me but it does. White trash is mean too."

"Seriously though, right? It's like anything different than their perfect little white world is offensive." Lauren sighed, "But I think it'll be different for Brittany. I mean, for one thing she'll have nice clothes and shit. That always helps."

Carrie and the kids came in, and the atmosphere in the house shifted with the happy, noisy sounds of kids playing and women chatting. Jaz already wished she could protect her own baby from racists, but she didn't think that was possible.

After Lauren and Brittany left and they had supper, Jaz asked Carrie if she could tell the kids about her pregnancy. "Of course! It's what you want?"

"Yeah, I'm starting to feel OK about it. I told Lauren today—well actually, she guessed—but it was nice that it wasn't a secret anymore."

"What's a secret?" Katie demanded, walking into the kitchen where Jaz and Carrie were chatting.

"Get your brother and we'll tell you."

"MATTHEW!!!! IT'S SECRET TIME!"

"I'm right here Katie, geez. Even the neighbors heard that one!" He walked in holding the controller for his game. "What's up?"

"So, I just wanted you guys to know that I'm pregnant. I'm going to have a baby!" She watched their faces carefully. Matthew opened his mouth, and then closed it again.

Katie wasn't so controlled, "Where's the daddy? You can't have a baby without the daddy!"

"Well, he decided he didn't want a baby. So he's not around."

"Oh," Katie thought for a minute, "Well, you shouldn't borrow my daddy because he's a meanie... I know! You can borrow Jonathan. He'd be a good daddy!"

Jaz looked over at Carrie and laughed to see her turn bright red. Clearly Katie wasn't the only one who thought Jonathan would make a good daddy! "Thanks Katie, but I'll be OK. What I really need are some kids to be my baby's special friends. Do you know of any?"

"YES, YES!" Katie jumped up and down and stuck her hand in the air, "Me, Princess Jasmine, me! Oh, and Matthew too. And Brittany! Cause she'll be big one day! Is that enough?"

Jaz felt her eyes getting hot, but this time the tears that threatened to come were tears of joy and gratitude, "Yeah, Katie, that's definitely enough. Thanks!"

Satisfied, the kids both turned back to their activities. Carrie surprised Jaz by gently grabbing her and giving her a big hug. "I'm so proud of you! You're going to be an amazing mom!"

Jaz quickly hugged her back before letting go. "I really wouldn't be OK without your help. Thank you."

CHAPTER 10

*J*az was almost finished working on her new upcycled pregnancy wardrobe. The chance to create her own things was something she looked forward to all day. One of her favorites was a jean jacket. Her mom refused to let her have one, even though she asked every year when she was in elementary school. Now that she was making her own choices, she was determined to have a jean jacket she could wear even when she started to show more.

At first, she planned to just have one she never buttoned up. But she didn't like how it draped. After making some sketches, she came up with a solution so weird that it just might work—she'd cut out the entire belly area, and finish the seams as if the jacket was always supposed to have 'space' for a baby belly. As long as her chest didn't get too big she could still do up the top three buttons. And maybe she could figure out how to repurpose the front of a zip up sweatshirt to fit into the jacket so she could cover her stomach when it got cooler.

She found lots of ideas online for pregnancy clothes that weren't lame, but she was pretty sure her jacket would be one-of-a-kind. For the first time ever, the idea of going out and *not* looking like everyone else made her happy.

Needing a break after behind hunched over the sewing machine struggling with the denim, she decided to go out for a walk. Grabbing her phone more out of habit than necessity, she said bye to Carrie. The kids were at the playground, but she didn't think they'd be too long. It was one of the hottest days in the summer. Thank goodness she had a nice cool basement to hang out in when she got back.

She was gaining confidence about taking walks and exploring. Now that her hair was so different, she was pretty sure she could pass her old friends and not be recognized. But what she really liked to do while she was walking was watch people, and try to re-imagine them in different clothes.

That mom in front of the townhouse wearing a long sleeve t-shirt and jeans and yelling at a bunch of kids? Jaz pictured her in a cute halter-top sundress. Something that made her feel pretty and nice.

The teen sitting on a bench hunched over his phone wearing a stretched out t-shirt that he kept pulling back when it slipped down at the neck? He deserved a bright green t-shirt with a cool image of a vintage video game.

And the elderly couple slowly walking up their driveway holding hands? Something fancier for them, that made them feel as special as they deserved for still being there for each other. Jaz was so lost in thought as she made her way back to the house that she didn't realize there was a stranger pounding on Carrie's front door and yelling until she was halfway up the path. She tried to walk away before he saw her but it was too late.

As soon as he saw movement out of the corner of his eye, he spun around. Jaz knew right away it was the ex-husband. He was like an old version of Matthew but with a puffy, red face, and baggy clothes.

"TELL ME WHERE CARRIE IS YOU LITTLE CHINK!"

Jaz instinctively raised up her hands and tried to think of some way to get him away from the house. Suddenly the door flew open and Carrie was there. She was standing as tall as she could, but Jaz could see her hands shaking.

"Leave her alone Don!"

"Well, well, well. If it isn't my pathetic wife. WHERE ARE MY KIDS CARRIE?"

"They're not here. You need to leave Don. This is completely unacceptable." Carrie leaned against the doorframe, and Jaz thought she saw her hand shaking.

"I'M NOT GOING UNTIL I HAVE THE KIDS. YOU CAN'T HIDE THEM FROM ME! I HAVE A RIGHT TO BE HERE, AND YOU'RE GOING TO BE REAL SORRY FOR BEING SUCH A BITCH!"

Immediately Jaz realized that all of Carrie's talk about boundaries and standing up for yourself had come from her own life. *Any time something doesn't feel right, take the action you need to take to keep yourself safe* she had said just the other day. Slowly Jaz reached into her back pocket and pulled out her phone. Carrie glanced her way and barely nodded. It was the confirmation Jaz needed.

She dialed 9-1-1 and carefully backed up, hoping not to catch his attention. In the background she was vaguely aware of Carrie standing firm and telling him to leave.

"Nine one one what's your emergency?"

"Police," Jaz whispered, "I need police right now."

"Alright, what's going on?"

"This man is at the front door. He's my friend's ex. He's yelling and screaming and oh my gosh I think he's going to start hitting her. Hurry!"

The calm voice at the other end seemed inappropriate, "What's your address?"

Jaz rattled it off and then noticed Jonathan running down the street in his bare feet. She breathed a sigh of relief. But instead of running right to Carrie, he stopped beside Jaz. Carrie gave him the quickest head shake. Jaz didn't understand. Why didn't she want him to help?

In the background she heard the dispatcher say the police were on their way. "Do you know the name of the man?"

Jaz couldn't think of his name, and she couldn't remember Carrie's last name. Her thoughts were interrupted by Don lifting up his arm at Carrie. She had to do something!

"The police are on their way Carrie!" she nearly shouted.

The man spun around to face her, and then realized she wasn't alone. He seemed to stop for a second, unsure of who to attack first. Carrie told him again to leave, and he stormed past them. Jaz heard the operator asking what was happening as he got into a black car and squealed away from the house. Suddenly Carrie was beside her with her phone out. She showed Jaz the license plate number she had typed out.

"He just drove away. His license plate is, um, YKT836 Um, here." She handed the phone to Carrie. Her hand was shaking so much she couldn't hold it to her ear anymore. She heard Carrie say the kids weren't at home, and felt the world turn blurry. Suddenly Carrie's arms were around her, holding her up. "Come on, let's get you sitting down. That was quite a terrible thing to experience."

Jaz collapsed on the sofa with Carrie's arm tight around her. She couldn't stop shaking. Never in her life had she witnessed someone yelling like that. It made her feel sick to her stomach. How on earth had Carrie ever been married to such a horrible person? And poor Matthew and Katie! They must be terrified of their dad.

"The police should be here soon," she told Carrie. "I wish I could have done something more to help." When the police came, a nice-looking officer sat down on the sofa beside her while Carrie and Jonathan went to the dining table with another officer.

Gently the officer asked her to tell what had happened while she took notes. Jaz forced herself to remember everything as best as she could but all she wanted was just to curl up in a ball and cry. She didn't realize she *was* crying until the lady passed the box of Kleenex to her.

"It's OK to cry, honey. But you have to know how brave and amazing you were to call 911 right away. Your friend's lucky to have someone so smart and capable looking out for her."

Jaz felt the tears slow, "Really?"

"Absolutely. Any time you're afraid because of someone else, calling us is the right thing to do. If we can get to situations like this quickly we can make a big difference. But it's people like you making the call that really save the day." She smiled at Jaz and held a business card out to her, "This has been pretty scary for you. If you need, you can call this toll free counseling number any time to talk about it. It's completely confidential."

Jaz took the card and thanked her. She wished she had known about that number months earlier when she had no one to talk to about being pregnant. But now she had Carrie, and that was way better.

Once the police left, Carrie and Jonathan sat with Jaz until she felt calm enough to get up and use the bathroom. When she came back, she asked where the kids were.

"They're at Jonathan's. We were just getting ready to go swimming when Don came. I managed to get the kids out the back door without him noticing and they ran to Jonathan's. Thank goodness he and his friend Chris were there. And you Jaz! You were amazing today. Thank you so much!"

"Will he come back?"

"I don't know. I guess it depends whether he's caught driving. His license is suspended because of drunk driving convictions. And I'm pretty sure he has to be on good behavior since he just got out of jail." Carrie sighed, "It's not something I know a lot about. I just know it was better for us when he was gone."

After a few more minutes Jaz turned to Carrie, "Are you going to get the kids?"

She smiled gently, "Only once I know you're alright. They're safe right now where they are."

"No, you should go see them now. I'm alright here. I'll just call the police again if I see anything."

"OK, lock the door behind us?"

"Definitely!"

For the whole time they were gone Jaz sat by the window with her phone in her hand. She wanted to make sure to warn Carrie if she saw anyone who looked like her ex. And she was ready to dial 911 again in a heartbeat. How on earth had Carrie survived being married to him?

When the four of them came back, Matthew was quieter than usual but Katie didn't seem to be upset at all. Her constant chatter covered up everyone else's silence while Jonathan ordered takeout and Carrie set the table. Jaz was happy to have Matthew sitting close beside her on the sofa while Katie jumped around the room.

The food was surprisingly good. Jaz hadn't eaten much real Chinese food since her ma ma died, and the takeout was as close as she'd had. It was comforting in a way. When she was younger and her mom worked shift work, she'd often stay for supper at ma ma's. She treasured those memories. Eating was sacred time when ma ma finally put down her work and gave Jaz her undivided attention. She never corrected her, either. Not like her mom.

Although everyone else was avoiding talking about what happened,

Katie jumped in as soon as they started eating.

"Mommy, did jail make Daddy a bad person?"

"No Katie. Your daddy chose to try and control people around him instead of facing the things inside of him that make him angry. And he made those choices long before he went to jail."

"Like when he made us leave his house in our pajamas and said he never wanted to see us again?"

Carrie visibly flinched, "Yeah. Instead of facing his own problem with not paying the rent, he tried to make you and Matthew upset."

"And you Mommy. He made you cry. I don't like that."

There was quiet for a few minutes before Jaz spoke up, "For Chinese food, this isn't bad."

Everyone laughed, lightening the mood a bit. "I lived in Singapore for a few years, and I've been working my way through every Asian restaurant here," said Jonathan. "So far this is the winner. I'm glad you sort of like it."

Jaz was still thinking about all the crap Carrie had dealt with. "I didn't know your ex was like that. I guess I thought all the advice you gave me was what you learned at school. But I guess today I realized you're strong because you choose to be. It's not just words to you. It's cool."

That evening Carrie reminded them all to spend time saying *I love myself* because it would help heal their hearts. Jaz would've forgotten about it, but found that it made a different in helping some of the stress from the day go away. She rubbed her tummy while she whispered the words, and imagined a warm bubble of safety encircling her and her baby. Her heart was broken over her parent's rejection but at least she didn't have to deal with a psycho ex-husband. It changed how she saw Carrie, too. If she could be doing so good now with everything that had happened to her and the kids, then maybe Jaz would be OK too.

CHAPTER 11

*J*az spent the evening downstairs sewing. The next morning she was up early, excited and eager to show Carrie what she was working on. It was a good thing she'd been working on some new clothes. She couldn't do up any of her old shorts anymore, and she was starting to spill out of her bras. It was embarrassing—and uncomfortable.

She put on a boho top that she had taken down a few sizes to fit her. Using the techniques her grandma taught her, she put darts below the bust that allowed room for her growing belly but lay mostly flat for now. Underneath she had on a pair of ripped jean shorts— another thing she had never been allowed to wear—but she had used a pattern she saw online to add in a stretchy panel of fabric on each side so she could continue to do them up. Everything came from the thrift store except the thread Carrie had told her to use from her sewing box.

The reaction she got from Carrie when she came upstairs was price- less. Jaz was pretty sure she had done well, but seeing how it impressed Carrie gave her a huge smile she couldn't wipe off her face. She ran downstairs and brought up everything else she made.

There were some vintage looking men's t-shirts that she had re-made to fit her, a few pairs of shorts with belly panels, and the jean jacket that Jaz was so proud of. The only clothes problem she couldn't solve on her own was bigger bras. Her mom had ordered all of their underwear online. Jaz hadn't ever been in a lingerie store, or even in the underwear section of a department store.

"Have you always been able to do this with clothes?"

"I never designed my own stuff, but I'm ok at sewing. I wish I would have taken a clothing design course at school. This was so much fun. I kinda forgot about all the bad stuff for a while."

Carrie smiled, "Jaz, I think you're on to something here."

"There's just one thing... I need your help."

"Of course! What is it? Wait, are you blushing?"

Jaz groaned and hid her face. "I need bigger bras," she mumbled from behind her hands.

"Well, they do say there's a first time for everything!"

"I don't even know where to go. My mom always bought them for me."

"Oh, I see. No problem. Hey, how about I see if Jonathan can take the kids for a bit tomorrow and you and I go to the mall together? You can wear your cool clothes and we'll go laugh at the cheesy preggo clothes before we get you some new underwear. You're going to need everything eventually."

"Cool! Thanks!"

The next day they all went to the mall. Jonathan wanted to take the kids mini golfing while Carrie and Jaz shopped, and then they'd all meet up for a late lunch.

As they walked past stores, Carrie kept raving about Jaz's clothes. Since the air conditioning was always cold in the mall, Jaz was already getting a chance to try out her new jacket. Every time she caught a glimpse of her reflection in a window she reminded herself that this really was her. With the new haircut, and a totally different style of clothes than she had ever imagined she could wear, she found herself smiling at the 'new' her.

"Seriously Jaz, the way you re-did that jacket is so cool. It's a lot like what Lauren does with her paintings. You know, repurposing things and making them way better than they were to start."

"Thanks! It took a while to figure out how to finish it after I cut out the center, but I like it too!" Spending so much time with Katie — who complimented herself as much as she complimented others — was rubbing off on Jaz. It felt good to say something she liked about herself.

When they got to the maternity store, Jaz could instantly see what Carrie meant. The clothes were full of ruffles, bows, and gathers that would hide any body shape a woman might actually have — pregnant or not. And there was definitely nothing that said 'cool' or 'pregnant and under thirty years old'.

Just as they were leaving, a lady came right up to Jaz. "I love your jacket! Where did you get it?"

"Oh, thank you. I made it."

"No way. It's the coolest maternity jacket I've ever seen."

The lady just kept standing there, and Jaz didn't know what else to say. Fortunately, Carrie did, "She repurposed it from a vintage jacket. And it has a removable fleece panel that can zip up over the belly for cool weather!"

"Are you kidding?" Waving over her friend, she turned Jaz to face her, "*LOOK* at this jacket! It's totally vintage. Don't you love it?"

Jaz was stunned. She had never in her life been pointed out for what she was wearing.

Again, Carrie saved the moment, "You know, she might be branching out into one-of-a-kind maternity clothes. Jaz, why don't you give them your Instagram handle. You'll be putting things up there, right?"

Jaz looked at her, confused. "Um, yeah. OK, it's at jazzy gurl—with two z's a 'u'—two point oh." She watched them both type it in and click 'follow'.

"Will you have anything this week? I'm getting *so* tired of this," with a dismissive wave, the other lady covered the entire maternity store.

"Yeah, maybe."

Fortunately Carrie steered Jaz out of the store before she said anything else lame. A few stores down, she stopped and turned to her, "What do you think Jaz? Feel like becoming a clothing designer?"

"I don't know. Do you really think they liked it?" She fingered the collar of her jacket self-consciously. After all, anyone could cut up a jean jacket! And those women were wearing head to toe name brands. They wouldn't be interested in old thrift store clothes… would they?

"Oh yeah. And with a few women like that wearing your stuff and sharing it on social media you could really go places! But it's up to you hon. At least you know that you are going to be the most stylin' momma-to-be in town! Now come on, I think there's a department store where we can get maternity underwear."

Jaz only half paid attention to Carrie while they found bras and underwear to fit her growing body. She was so caught up in what just happened that she forgot to be embarrassed. While she tried on bras, she remembered a conversation she had had with her mom after spending the weekend with ma ma. She must've been ten or eleven.

"Mommy, when I grow up I want to be just like ma ma."

"You mean old, and living in a tiny apartment?"

"No! I want to make clothes just like she does! Today this lady came in and she had this beautiful dress that didn't fit her, and ma ma's going to—"

"Enough Jasmine! Your grandmother selfishly insists on staying in that hovel and slaving over white people's clothes because she is too stubborn to live here with us like she should. You will study hard and become a doctor. No more foolish wishes!"

"But mommy—" A sharp look from her mom shut her up instantly. The next statement from her mom terrified her.

"If I hear one more word about anything other than being a doctor, you will never see your grandmother again. Go to your room. You are not to come out until it is time for school tomorrow."

Jaz had quietly gone to her room and stayed there until the morning. As soon as her mom left for her morning run, she had dashed to the bathroom, nearly having an accident on the way.

Giving her head a shake, Jaz carefully hung up the bras she didn't like before getting dressed and leaving the change room. It made her wonder, though, whether she really could turn the most special times she had shared with ma ma into a career that could provide for her baby.

Over lunch with Jonathan and the kids they talked about the possibility of Jaz selling clothes online. Carrie had insisted on paying her for helping with the *Framed* business, so she was already making some money, but Jaz had to admit, working on the clothes made her happier than she could have imagined. It would be amazing to sell what *she* designed.

CHAPTER 12

"*H*ave you looked at what you need to earn to support you and your baby?" Carrie looked up from the frame she was painting. Jaz stopped mid-post, surprised. She had just updated all the *Framed* social media feeds.

"No, not really…" She sent the last post and closed her laptop. Money had never been a problem for her, and even now with the money Carrie gave her every week she hadn't really thought about anything she'd need later.

"It may seem a little cold-hearted," Carrie continued gently, "But the thing is, you're the only one your baby can rely on. Since there isn't support coming in from anywhere else, it's up to you to provide everything. And even if you did get some financial help, it can become a trap if you have no way of making it financially on your own."

"I guess it's just never been an issue for me. I mean, I know there's poor people out there, but I've always been OK." Awareness began to creep through her body, and it wasn't a nice feeling. "My parents used to take care of everything. But I didn't think about doing that for my own baby…"

"OK, well why don't you start by writing down the things you think you'll need and how much they'll cost. And if you want I can show you my budget and we can talk some more. Us women are pretty amazing at working things out when we set our minds to it."

Just then Lauren came in with more paintings for sale. After they enjoyed looking through them, they sat at the table. "Cool outfit! Gee, way back when I was pregnant they sure didn't have clothes like this!"

Jaz was wearing a soft grey t-shirt that she had altered to be a summer dress. It wasn't anything special, but she had added a V-neck collar and white stripes down each side. What she really liked was how cool and comfortable it was. She liked Lauren, and felt like she could talk to her about things — even money.

"Thanks! Hey, how much does her stuff cost?" She nodded her head towards Brittany. "I mean, how much do you need to have for a baby?"

Lauren didn't seem surprised by the question, "Well, at first we hardly had money for anything and it was super hard. I'd keep her in a diaper as long as possible before changing her so I wouldn't run out, and we were all sleeping on the floor. Then Carrie gave me the job doing frames, and Kara gave us all her baby stuff. Things got better after that. I guess you can survive with just a bit of money. But it sucks big time. I'd never have another baby if I didn't have money now." She looked up at Jaz, "Oh, sorry. I didn't mean you. I mean... shit."

"No, it's OK. I just never thought about it. Like, what I should do next. I've never even had a real job. My parent's said it would impact my grades so I wasn't allowed to."

"I worked at McDonald's until I got pregnant. But now, getting paid to paint? It rocks. And I don't have to leave Brittany to go to work. That's really the best part. Well that and the crap load of money coming in!"

The talk turned to an end of summer barbeque that Carrie wanted to have before her school started again. Jaz was shocked to hear Lauren complain about how busy Carrie would be. She had just assumed things would continue like they had in the summer.

Lauren hadn't really given Jaz an answer about how much it cost to have a baby. Looking around, Jaz started to wonder how things would work out for her. Sure, Carrie's kids were older, but they had their own rooms, clothes, and toys. Not to mention food. The last time Carrie went grocery shopping Jaz had joined her. The $118 hadn't seemed like a lot, but Carrie mentioned that her budget used to be $40. Jaz's mom could spend ten times that at Costco.

"I wish I had clothes like this," Katie sighed dramatically, interrupting Jaz's thoughts later on that evening. She had used scrap fabric to make some fun clothes for Katie's dolls, and the two of them were sitting on the floor dressing them up.

"Hey!" Carrie called from the kitchen, "You've got more clothes than ever before Katie-girl. And we'll get you some fun clothes when we go back to school shopping in a few days."

"I know, but these clothes are *special*. Not like the boring ones at the store."

Ideas flew through Jaz's head faster than she could track them, and all thoughts of budgets and planning for the future vanished.

"What about you Matthew?" she asked.

"Huh?" he mumbled into his controller.

"Do you like your clothes?"

"Well…" he looked at Carrie as she walked into the living room with a mug of coffee.

She smiled, but not her usual big sunny smile, "I already know, bud. It's OK to say it out loud."

"Sorry Mom, but I don't really like the clothes you buy me. Some stuff is OK. Like that dress shirt I wore for Christmas not last year but the year before."

Jaz got out her phone and went to sit beside him. After a few seconds of typing, she showed him her screen. Using some search terms for cool and unique boys' clothes she quickly found a variety of ideas. "What about this stuff?"

"Cool! Yeah, I like that. And this one with the bow tie? I mean, I wouldn't wear it to school. But I like it. There's no clothes like this where we shop."

Jaz was surprised that he liked something so unusual. She hadn't seen any boys his age dressing up for anything. They looked through pictures together for a while, and she got a pretty good idea of his style. Unique and original clothes that had interesting patterns, but nothing too flashy or outrageous. And he'd definitely prefer to dress up more than he could with his current wardrobe.

By the time they were done looking through the pictures she knew what she'd do. Using the money Carrie was paying her, she'd buy clothes from the thrift store and convert them into the perfect style for Matthew, Katie, and Carrie. Jaz knew that the tired clothes they wore most of the time didn't reflect their personal styles at all, and she was pretty sure it was something she could change for them.

Now that her own 'new' maternity wardrobe was pretty much done she missed having projects. Whether she'd admit it or not, years of being told to work harder no matter what she was doing had become an ingrained part of her life. She might not be studying anymore, but she had to do *something.*

The perfect chance to get supplies turned up a few days later. Carrie had planned an end-of-summer barbeque and Jonathan was coming over to help get things ready. Jaz had already offered to help a few times, but Carrie insisted everything was under control.

The thrift stores were too far away to walk, so Jaz looked up how to take the bus. Her parents refused to let her take public transportation, believing it was too dangerous. They had either driven her wherever she needed to go, or used a private hire service that their friend's parents used for their kids. When she turned sixteen they paid for lessons until she passed her driver's test, but she rarely needed to drive anywhere, even after that. She never appreciated the convenience of always having a ride when she wanted until now.

When she successfully got off the bus at the right stop she silently congratulated herself. With her new haircut, new clothes, and new transportation options she was starting to feel like she was growing up.

At the thrift store she grabbed one of the few shopping carts and began making her way through the store. One rack at a time, she looked for clothes that were the right fabric and color. Style and size didn't matter at all — she'd take care of that herself.

The only thing she couldn't find was the type of shoes she had in mind to go with some of the kid's outfits she planned. She hoped Carrie was planning on buying them new shoes for fall that would work OK. Her mom had drilled into her the importance of always putting together an entire outfit, including the right shoes.

Jaz paused for a moment as a wave of homesickness washed over her. Her mom had been strict, demanding, and often cold, but she taught Jaz so many things that she was using now. If only she could accept that Jaz was still her daughter, even though she made a mistake. She missed her dad less, but she wished she could show him what she was doing, and let him know she was OK. In his quiet way he had been so proud of her accomplishments. But she supposed re-doing clothes from the thrift store wouldn't exactly impress either of her parents.

Bracing herself, she turned back to the clothes rack. Surprisingly, there were three different jean jackets in the ladies section. Jaz checked to make sure they were in decent condition, and then added all three to the cart. When she made it to the cashier the total was a shocking $157.49. How had a bunch of two and three dollar items added up to all that? Feeling worried, she used her bank card to pay for everything and then waited while the cashier put everything into three big bags.

She was subdued on the bus ride home. Her bank account had less than $20 in it now. She had checked a few nights ago, hoping her parents had put more money in. They hadn't, and now she was out of money except for the $50 Carrie would give her at the end of the week. What was she supposed to do now?

It wasn't until she quickly went downstairs with her bags and tucked them in the furnace room out of the way that she remembered the jean jackets. If those pregnant woman at the store in the mall were actually interested, she could re-do the jackets and sell them. It would be a lot to get done because she didn't have much time before the kids went back to school and she wanted them to have their new clothes. She couldn't wait until Carrie's dinner was over so she could set up the sewing machine in the basement and get started!

CHAPTER 13

*C*arrie's barbeque was nothing like Jaz had ever experienced before. The few times her parents hosted dinner parties they always hired a chef to do the cooking. For days before her mom would stress about the table settings, the menu, and the guests. By the time the dinner was due to start she was always a bundle of nerves. Jaz spent those evenings in her room, being as quiet as possible.

But here, the entire house seemed to be alive with adults laughing, kids tearing around, and people hugging, drinking and helping set out the food. Jonathan stationed himself at Carrie's new barbeque until he was kicked out by his brother Max who claimed he was killing the meat. As an only child Jaz found their interactions fascinating, and found herself staring at them, wondering what it would have been like to have a sibling.

All of Carrie's friends took the time to talk to Jaz, and the women were thrilled by her trendy maternity clothes. Her outfit was a former men's short-sleeved white dress shirt with little blue sailboats over it, that she converted it into a cute summer dress with a matching fabric belt and little cap sleeves with a notch on each side.

Right now she used the belt to cinch the dress in over her modest baby bump, but there was definitely a lot more room for her belly when she needed it. Their feedback gave her confidence that Carrie's idea for selling clothes might be a good one.

Jaz just sat down on the couch with a Coke after making sure she had visited with everyone—another thing her mom had made her do in social situations—when Carrie's old landlord Mr. Morris arrived.

"No, no, don't get up," he insisted, seeing her start to stand up, "I spent the day working in my little garden so I'm quite happy to sit beside you. I'm Henry Morris by the way. I used to be Carrie's land-lord, and she's nice enough to keep inviting me over."

"Hi, I'm Jaz." Normally she kept her conversations short with strangers, but there was something about this kind-looking man that seemed to draw the words out of her. "I'm living with Carrie because I'm pregnant and my parents kicked me out."

"Oh my dear, I'm so sorry. That must be terribly difficult, although I imagine Carrie is the perfect person to live with in a tricky situation. Do you mind me asking when you're due?"

"Middle of February. I'll know more in a few weeks."

"Ah, that will be lovely! My boy was born February sixth, nine-teen sixty-five. I loved nothing better than taking him out when the weather warmed up and showing him off to everyone." He chuckled at the memory and his eyes crinkled at the corners. "My wife told me I'd spoil him with all the attention, but he turned out just fine. He lives in Australia now, with his wife and his two sons."

"What about your wife?"

His face dropped, and Jaz felt bad for asking, "My wife passed away seven years ago. Dementia. She didn't even recognize me, but I like to think she was still happy to the end."

"Oh, I'm sorry. That's terrible." Jaz had never heard of someone dying from dementia. "My grandma died four years ago. She got the flu and then pneumonia. But at least she always knew who I was."

They sat beside each other in silence then, watching all the action around them. Jaz was glad he didn't feel he needed to keep asking her questions. When Katie saw the two of them she ran over and climbed into Jaz's lap before leaning over to give Mr. Morris a hug.

"Mister Morris! I'm so HAPPY you're here! Isn't our new house BEEEEAUTIFUL? And have you met my Princess Jasmine? She cut her hair, but she's still a princess!"

"Yes, my dear. I've had the pleasure of meeting Princess Jasmine. You sure are lucky to live with a princess!"

"Yep!" she nodded, "And she's going to have a baby princess too! She's right here!" Katie rubbed Jaz's belly for a few seconds before leaning down to kiss it and then jumping up and running back to her friends.

Carrie called everyone to come and eat, and Jaz and Mr. Morris were happy to get caught up in the crowd of people filing past the food set out on the table. Dustin was just ahead of her and she watched as he deftly set his plate down, used his good hand to fill it, and then picked it up again. He made his way outside where Carrie had discretely set up a small table and one of the wooden chairs from the kitchen. Lauren was waiting for him, and she set Brittany beside him before going to get food for herself and Brittany. Jaz was amazed at the way the couple seemed to navigate around his issues without a problem.

After eating her fill and then having some trifle that Jenny had brought for dessert, Jaz was uncomfortably full. She wandered through the backyard to stretch her legs before relaxing in an empty lawn chair.

"Lisa, right?" she asked, turning to the lady beside her.

"Right! Good memory! I can remember you're Jaz, but that's because you're the only new person I met today."

"I'm sorry, but I don't remember your mom's name." Jaz looked apologetically to the lady beside Lisa.

"That's alright, I'm Maria. We were just talking about how lovely Carrie's place is. Did you ever see her old place?"

"Um, no I didn't."

"Well you're not missing much. Such a drab, worn down place. I know she did her best there, but this house is way more suited to her!"

Jaz nodded her agreement. She couldn't imagine Carrie living anywhere else.

"So Jaz, what will you be doing this fall?"

The question from Lisa surprised her for a moment. "Well, I'm not quite sure. Carrie has been great to let me live here, but we haven't really talked about how long." She put a hand on her stomach, "My baby's due in February. I guess I have to figure some stuff out still."

"What would you most love to do?"

"Oh, that's easy! Make clothes!" Jaz could see they were both nodding politely, but had no idea what she was talking about. "See, Carrie introduced me to thrift stores and they're full of all these super cheap clothes with so much potential! Like this dress. It used to be a men's shirt!"

"No!" Lisa gasped. She reached out and fingered the tidy notch on the sleeve. "It's finished perfectly! And the whole idea to turn a man's shirt into a dress? That's beyond incredible! You could sell this!"

"Yeah," Jaz leaned forward, feeling excitement fill her for the second time that day, "That's what I was thinking. Carrie and I ran into some pregnant ladies at the mall who loved this jean jacket I altered. They're following me on Instagram now, and I found some jackets today that I'm going to fix up and try to sell. I have SO many ideas!"

They were both curious about where Jaz leaned to sew, and she told them all about her grandma and the happy times they spent together.

"What a sweet memory!" Lisa replied, "My grandma passed away when I was quite young. You're so fortunate to have had those times. And now you can use everything she taught you! I bet she'd be so proud of you."

"I hope so. I don't know though. When my parents found out I was pregnant they were so mad. They haven't talked to me since. Thank goodness for Carrie taking me in. But I wonder if ma ma would have been just as angry at me."

Lisa and Maria exchanged a glance. "Never give up hope," Maria counseled, "Every relationship has a chance to heal, I promise you that."

"Thanks. I really miss them."

"You know, staying in Carrie's basement isn't the best long-term plan. Have you thought about other options?"

Jaz shook her head no. They were right. She couldn't just stay living with Carrie. It wouldn't be fair to her and the kids, especially if she had to work as hard at her university courses as Lauren claimed.

"I have an idea," Lisa interrupted her thoughts, "I've got a pretty big house that Mom and I live in. We've had my friend Amy living in one of the rooms, but she got married last month so she's moved out. That bedroom shares a bathroom with a guestroom we rent out on Airbnb. And there's another room that would be perfect for sewing in. It has a south-facing window, so it gets lots of natural light."

Jaz felt her mouth hanging open, but she couldn't think of anything intelligent to say.

"I think you're in a tough place and I'd like to help you out." Lisa continued, "And Mom would love to have that room occupied again. She starts to wilt when she's not around people!" Her eyes twinkled as she looked at Maria, who waved her hand in the air with a laugh.

"But I don't have any money right now."

"I think you're going to do quite well financially once you get your business going. There's no pressure from me, because I've already learned from Carrie how important it is for each person to make the best choices for their own life."

Jaz nodded, "Yeah, that sounds like something Carrie's been saying to me since the day I moved in."

"If you'd like, you could try it out for a month at no charge, and then if you want to stay we can work out a fair rate for rent once your business picks up."

"Seriously? You'd do that for me?"

"Definitely! Mom and I are big believers in paying it forward. So if this helps you out then all I ask is that you help someone else out when you get the chance."

"Wow! That's… that's just really cool. Thank you. I, um, I'd like to try staying with you. But…"

"It's OK, nothing you say will hurt my feelings!"

"Well, it's not really about you. It's just that I'd like to spend a bit more time here first. They've kinda become my family and I feel like it's going to be hard to leave." Jaz found tears welling up in her eyes, "Oh boy, I thought I was over the whole crying thing. Sorry. I cry a lot when people are nice to me."

Maria reached across Lisa and held Jaz's hand gently. "You're a sweet, sweet girl. Never apologize for that!"

CHAPTER 14

*J*az stood at the bottom of the basement stairs and looked around her. She had been so anxious to get started on her plan that it had been agony to wait for Carrie's friends to leave and then help clean up. Finally, she felt like she could excuse herself and come downstairs.

All the things she bought from the thrift store were now laid out across the floor and the sofa. She wanted to see everything before deciding what to tackle first. Should she work on things to sell first or things for Carrie and the kids?

She went to the jean jackets and made a small pile with the medium sized one on the top. That would fit either of the ladies she met at the mall so that would be the first 'for sale' one she did. Then she went through and made stacks for Matthew, Katie, and Carrie. When she was done, all of them would have a couple of re-made outfits, plus some extra tops. Jaz was so excited she felt her heart beating faster.

Taking the short-sleeve white dress shirt from Matthew's pile, she decided to start there. She sat at the table and began taking the collar off and removing the buttons. Then she took a blue paisley men's shirt and made a pattern using the collar. Next she cut strips of the same fabric to cover the panel where the buttons went and the top of the pocket. An hour later Jaz was ironing the finished shirt—thank goodness Carrie stored her iron and ironing board downstairs!

Jaz held up the shirt and smiled. It definitely said 'Matthew'. The collar was now the bright blue paisley, along with a strip on the top of the pocket, and the panel behind the buttons let some of the same color peek through. She wanted to put the fabric along the panel that held the button holes, but it would take too long for this time. The final touch was a bow tie that she found in a bin at the thrift store. It was the exact blue as the accent on the paisley fabric so all Jaz had to do was make it smaller to fit a boy's neck.

She set the shirt with the bow tie tucked into the collar on the back of the sofa and moved on to jeans. The other day when Carrie was busy with Katie, Jaz had asked Matthew to try on his favorite jeans for her. They had fit well around the waist still, but were clearly too short. Now she used them as a template to redo a longer, cooler pair for him. She'd found a pair of skinny jeans at the thrift store that were almost brand new but too long. All she needed to do was shorten them, and bring them in a bit from the knees down to still fit right. It was something she had watched ma ma do over and over— hemming pants—and she smiled as she repeated the actions she watched so carefully when she was younger.

The rest of Matthew's clothes were pretty easy. A pair of khaki shorts that just needed a button sewn on and a hole in the front fixed. Jaz used the same paisley fabric to make a patch. Then she took the three t-shirts she found in the men's section and got to work on them. The first had a screen print of a vintage Nintendo controller on the front. The shirt was stained at the bottom so she cut out the print and sewed it onto a plain t-shirt in Matthew's size. The other two t-shirts just needed to be taken in to fit his slim torso. To add interest, she made a contrasting pocket for each of them.

Katie's outfits were next. First on the list was making her a pink, sparkly dress. The fabric had caught Jaz's eye, and she knew right away it was perfect. Sure, it was a curtain right now, but there was enough fabric there to make at least two dresses. Jaz had grabbed one of Katie's dresses that still fit her, and she used it as a pattern to cut the curtain.

The dress would be a simple short-sleeved shift, and then Jaz would gather the waist in to give it shape and add fabric to make the skirt flowy just the way Katie liked it. But before she gathered the waist she added a rainbow of ribbons that started at the right shoulder, and fell at an angle to the bottom of the dress on the left side. The ribbons were in the same bin that Jaz had found Matthew's bow tie in at the thrift store, and she figured she could use them in all sorts of ways.

The only thing missing from the outfit was some knee length socks. When Katie was showing Jaz her clothes the other day she confided in her that she 'hated wearing tights'. But Jaz thought the outfit would be adorable if she got some long white socks and put little matching rainbows on each side. She'd have to pick up some new ones tomorrow.

Jaz finished off her whirlwind sewing spree by embellishing some skirts and t-shirts for Katie. There was a lot more choice at the thrift store for girls' clothes that were still in decent shape and it was easy to add bows, sparkle, and frills to the clothes. In no time they were transformed into one-of-a-kind items that Jaz knew Katie would love.

She set everything out on the sofa and stepped back to get a good look. It was so much fun to make clothes for the kids. She couldn't wait until she had her own baby to style up! With a yawn and a stretch Jaz wandered over to check the time on her phone. Four in the morning!

"Holy cow!" she whispered. It felt like time had stood still while she was sewing. She was dying to get started on something for Carrie but was suddenly exhausted. It was all she could do to clean every-thing up and hide the clothes before she set out her bed on the floor and fell asleep.

CHAPTER 15

*J*az was up by eight the next morning, keen to keep sewing. It was all she could do to keep her projects to herself while she sat across from Carrie at the table drinking her tea. Fortunately Carrie was absorbed in something on her computer, so Jaz didn't interrupt her. Looking through the selfies she had taken in her own re-done maternity clothes she decided they were good enough to post on her Instagram feed. They had been taken using the mirror on the back of the bathroom door.

The picture of her in her jean jacket had been liked more than seventy times already, and there seemed to be new comments every day. Jaz decided to put aside Carrie's clothes for now and get a jacket done that she could sell. At least she had done one already, and learned through trial and error how to make the next one go a little quicker. By the afternoon it was almost done and Jaz's back and neck were aching from being hunched over the sewing machine all day.

She decided to take a break and walk to the nearest stores to get socks for Katie's outfit. If she finished it all today she could show it to Carrie tomorrow morning. Despite her sore body Jaz was tempted to skip down the road. The happiness she felt from spending the day (and the night before) creating was something she had never felt before. She rubbed her belly as she walked. If it wasn't for her pregnancy she'd be getting ready to go to university right now. It was hard to imagine how different her life might have been, and she couldn't picture *not* being able to sew every day.

After she found the socks she wanted for Katie she wandered over to the baby section. Lauren had talked about how hard it was to have a baby and no money, but Jaz thought she'd be OK. All she had to do was sell enough clothes to pay for the things she needed. And renting a room from Lisa couldn't be *that* expensive.

She stopped short when she got to the diapers. Sometimes Lauren had to change Brittany twice just during the time she was at Carrie's. So Jaz calculated she might go through a package or two *a week*. And that was just the diapers. Slowly she walked up and down the aisles, trying to add up how much she might spend. When she got to the baby furniture she sat down on one of the rocking chairs and took a shaky breath.

Carrie had hinted that Jaz's expenses could go up quite a bit in the future, but Jaz had brushed it off without much thought. Now she realized Carrie had been trying to gently prepare her. She rubbed her hand along the arm of the rocking chair. It felt like cheap crap and it squeaked when she rocked it just a little. Sure Lisa had offered her a deal, and even no rent to start, but Jaz still had to pay for everything for her baby.

Her mind wandered back through her own childhood. Gymnastics, dance, skating lessons, the best preschool in the city, vacations, name brand clothes, university tuition... Jaz wanted her baby to have everything she had. Well that, *and* to feel loved unconditionally. Like how Carrie treated her kids.

Her buzzing phone interrupted her thoughts. She quickly answered, "Hey Carrie!"

"Hey, we're about to eat supper. Just wondering if you're joining us."

"Oh my gosh. I didn't realize what time it was. I am SO sorry! I was just doing some shopping and—"

Carrie's laugh interrupted her, "—no worries! You're a grown woman and entitled to a life! Do you want me to set a plate aside for you?"

"Yes please. And I'm so sorry for losing track of time." Jaz couldn't believe it. At home, missing dinner was inexcusable.

"It's really OK Jaz. Enjoy your time out!"

Jaz hung up the call still feeling bad. She paid for the socks and started to walk back to Carrie's. The bus would be faster, but suddenly she was worried about spending any money—even bus fare. If she couldn't sell clothes and make enough money to live on, she was in trouble and her baby would suffer.

After eating the dinner Carrie had left out for her, Jaz excused herself and went downstairs to sew. Suddenly, her fun idea for making clothes and selling them had become essential to her survival. She didn't know what else she could possibly do to earn a living.

It was after midnight when she finished the jacket, but already it was easier than the first one she had done. Tomorrow she'd try to work up the nerve to ask Carrie if she might model it—with a pillow in her shirt to make her look pregnant! It was too big for Jaz to model. Then, she'd post it on Instagram as her first item for sale.

Even though it was late, Jaz lay awake for quite a while. Ideas for different adaptations to clothes were flying through her head, along with calculations about how much she could charge, and how much she could earn in a week.

CHAPTER 16

*A*s soon as she heard Carrie in the kitchen, Jaz went upstairs to join her. She was sitting at the table with her coffee, looking dejected with her head in her hand.

"What's wrong?"

Carrie looked up, but was missing her usual morning smile for Jaz, "Oh, just dreading back-to-school shopping. I mean, it's OK. It's not like before when we had to register with a charity to get supplies and the kids were stuck with whatever clothes they already had. I shouldn't complain I guess. I just don't want to do it."

Jaz couldn't have picked a more perfect time to show what she had been working on, "Oh good, I have something for you then. But I also have something to tell you..." She hesitated, not sure if Carrie wanted to listen to her.

"Take your time! I'd much rather sit here with you than go get stuff done." Carrie took another sip of her coffee and smiled.

With a deep breath, she started, "I'm really, really glad you let me stay here. It's been...uh...you *are* like a big sister. I've always wanted that. And I love your kids." Again, she felt her eyes start to get hot. Why did she always cry when she thought about nice people?

"They love you too!"

"I know, and I want to still see them lots. But I've decided to move out."

Carrie looked shocked, but quickly tried to hide it. "Tell me more!"

"Well the other night at your party I was talking to Lisa. And she's got this room empty because her friend just got married and moved out."

"You're going to live with Lisa?" Jaz nodded. "Oh Jaz, that's wonderful! I don't want you to move out, but if you go anywhere else, I'd choose Lisa."

Jaz felt a weight fall off her shoulders to know that Carrie approved of her plan. "Yeah, she's pretty nice. And she's got an extra room that I can use to do my sewing and she said I only need to pay rent for it if I start to make money on my designs."

"Wow! So you're moving out *and* starting your business?"

She couldn't help but beam at the thought of having her own business, "Uh huh! I've had a ton of followers since I started putting up those maternity outfits I made for myself. You were right, everyone's going to be crazy to get clothes that are actually cool. And there's something else. But I need to wait until your kids are up."

Right on cue, Matthew came slowly down the stairs. Carrie smiled, "He'll be awake in about half an hour."

Jaz tried to be patient, but she could hardly wait to see what the kids and Carrie thought of the clothes.

After breakfast, everyone was finally awake enough for Jaz to get started. "OK, so Carrie, you need to go sit on the couch and wait for us. Katie and Matthew, come with me."

The followed Jaz downstairs, where she had set out all the kids' new clothes.

"Shhhhh," she warned, "I want these to be a surprise for your mom. Matthew, these are for you. And Katie, these are for you! What do you think!"

"I LOOOOOOOVE them!" Katie stage-whispered immediately, and then clapped her hand over her mouth and giggled. She went straight to the sparkly dress, just as Jaz had suspected. "Princess Jasmine! This is a real princess dress but it's my size! And the rainbow makes it the best ever!" With the dress still in her hand she turned and hugged Jaz's legs so tightly she almost lost her balance.

Matthew slowly went through each item of clothing, picking them up, turning them over, and then carefully setting them down again. He turned to Jaz. "Are they really mine?"

"Yeah, if you like them…"

"They're the nicest clothes ever. Nicer than the ones we saw on your phone! Can I try them on?"

"You bet! I thought maybe you could each pick an outfit to try on and surprise your mom with?" Suddenly Jaz felt nervous. What if the clothes didn't fit, or Carrie didn't like them?

"Cool!" Matthew breathed. He held up the dress shirt and skinny jeans. "Can I wear these?"

"Of course! Whatever you want! Katie, how about you?"

"The princess dress!"

"OK, and look, these are matching socks for the dress. That way you don't have to wear tights."

Katie's eyes sparkled as she held the socks up to the dress to look at the rainbows all together. "I'm going to be pretty!"

Jaz sat on the edge of the couch and looked Katie in the eye, "You've always been pretty Katie, cause your heart is pretty!"

For a moment Katie seemed to think about what she had just heard. "OK! Let's go change! Hide the clothes from Mommy!" In a flash she had gathered all her things and ran up the stairs.

Matthew carefully picked up his outfit and Jaz gathered everything else and followed them up the stairs. When they came out of their rooms all dressed up, she felt like jumping up and down and clapping. They looked awesome!

"OK, wait here until I call you. Katie, can you let Matthew go first?" Katie bit her lip in disappointment, and then nodded her agreement.

Jaz joined Carrie on the couch. "Are you ready for the world's most stylish kids? Because here they come!"

Matthew practically strutted down the stairs, and Jaz had to bite her cheeks to stop from smiling too big. He looked so proud and confident. The white newly-designed dress shirt and trendy jeans were perfect, and he could definitely pull off the bow tie too!

"Pretty cool, huh mom? It's even better than the pictures I saw on Jaz's phone!"

"Me next!" Katie called from the top of the stairs. She skipped down the stairs before giving a big twirl and then running to hug Jaz. "I'm so BEAUTIFUL!"

Carrie hadn't said anything yet, but her brilliant smile assured Jaz that she wasn't upset.

"Jaz, I'm amazed! It's like you somehow managed to put the kids' personalities into their clothes! They couldn't be dressed more perfectly!"

"Well, they still need shoes. I couldn't do that without your help. And I have a few cool t-shirts and a pair of shorts for Matthew for school, plus some skirts and tops for Katie. I just wanted you to see these ones first."

"I don't know how I can ever thank you for this!"

"Can I use them as models? For my Instagram page? These clothes are theirs to keep. But when I do more, I'd like them to model the clothes. I'm going to charge a lot for them. My mom would pay almost anything to have me wearing the 'right' things for school, so I just need to find other moms like her."

"Where did you get the fabric?"

Jaz smiled proudly, "You really have to ask?"

"NO! You did not! I'm in those stores every week! There's no way this stuff was all there!"

"Well, not *exactly* these clothes. But the original stuff all came from thrift stores. Matthew's jeans were close to the right size, so I just change them to be like skinny jeans but more comfortable. And Katie's dress was a curtain, so that was pretty easy. Oh, her socks I bought new and just added the rainbows. If you tell me what else they need for school clothes I can get it done before they start school. And before I move."

Tears filled Katie's eyes, "You're moving?"

Jaz crouched down awkwardly beside Katie. Her belly was definitely starting to change how she moved, "I am. It's time for you to have your mommy to yourself again. And I need to get ready to have my own baby."

"But I wanted you to have your baby HERE!" she wailed.

"I promise I'll bring him over every week to visit, OK?" Jaz had no idea how she would manage, but she was determined not to let Katie down, or to let these kids forget her.

Katie sniffed and nodded, "OK, but it's a her not a him."

Jaz turned to Carrie, "Could I come with you to pick out shoes? I have a look in mind. And then I want to use the pictures of the kids in these outfits for my page."

"Of course! Jaz, you're doing it! You're making your own path. I'm so proud of you, and so happy we know you. And I'm *so* grateful you saved me from shopping for clothes!"

Jaz was started to feel uncomfortable with all Carrie's praise. "I'm going to make some stuff for you too. I just wanted to get the kids' done before you went shopping."

"That is really good news. I hereby dub thee the master of my image!" She gave a mock bow.

Katie giggled. "You're silly."

Matthew left to show Jonathan his new outfit before changing back into play clothes. Carrie and Katie went up to look at the rest of Katie's new clothes, and Jaz sat back on the couch. She *was* really doing it! Maybe ma ma would be disappointed that she was pregnant, but Jaz knew she'd be proud of her for using all the things she had taught her granddaughter. And maybe once she was supporting herself with her business she could prove to her parents that they could still be proud of her too.

CHAPTER 17

By the end of the week Jaz had deposited the money from her first two sales into her bank account. Carrie encouraged her to keep careful track of how much she spent and earned with her business, and to try to put as much in the bank as possible.

The first jean jacket sold for $95, so Jaz spent another night doing up the second one, which also sold right away. Jaz loved seeing the ladies' face when they came to pick them up. Each one was so proud of her one-of-a-kind jacket, but Jaz knew all their pregnant friends would be wanting one just the same. She had her work cut out for her.

While at the thrift store looking for more jackets and items to convert to maternity clothes Jaz found a large green dress that was the perfect color for Carrie. On a whim, she grabbed a silver scarf too. That night instead of re-making a jean jacket, she turned the dress into a wrap dress in Carrie's size, and added a silver accent along the neckline and the hem.

After breakfast the next morning she brought up the dress, "This is the first new outfit for you."

"Oh my goodness Jaz, it's stunning!"

"The only thing is that you have to wear it on a date with Jonathan before I move."

Immediately Carrie began to blush, although she was already running her hand along the arm of the dress, "Oh, I don't know…"

Jaz pulled it out of reach, "No date, no dress! And I'll babysit, so there's no excuse not to go out."

Matthew looked as embarrassed as Carrie, but Katie was already clapping her hands, "Yay! Mommy and Uncle Johnny!"

With an exaggerated sigh, Carrie agreed.

"Call him up!" Jaz insisted.

"What, now?"

Jaz looked at the kids, "I think your mommy needs a little help."

"You should do it Mom." Matthew smiled, "Jonathan totally wants to."

Carrie covered her face with her hands, "I can't ask him out!"

"I will!" Katie volunteered.

"Aw, thanks Katie-girl. But maybe it's better if I do. Just this once though!"

As Jaz suspected, Jonathan immediately agreed to take Carrie out the next night for dinner. She didn't have his number so she had Matthew take a message to him telling him that Carrie would be all dressed up. She didn't want Carrie to have any reason to change out of the dress!

They worked on frames for the morning, and in the afternoon Jaz joined Carrie to shop for shoes for the kids. She insisted Carrie buy a cute pair of white heels to finish off her dress, and then wandered off on her own to buy silver dangly earrings and some bangles that would finish off Carrie's date night outfit.

After the kids were in bed, Carrie and Jaz sat in the living room chatting.

"I really can't thank you enough for the kids' new clothes, and that gorgeous dress for me. It's the nicest thing I've ever owned."

"Didn't you have a wedding dress?" It was obvious to Jaz that the memory of her wedding wasn't a happy one, and she immediately regretted asking.

"My parents wanted to buy my dress, but money was really tight for them so I pushed for a casual wedding so I could just wear something inexpensive. It was still nice, but nothing special. Of course, it's not like it was the start of anything good."

"Do you want to get married again?" Marriage wasn't really something Jaz thought about. There had always been an expectation that she would have a career first, and then marry someone her parents approved of.

"Maybe. It's taken a few years for me to recover from my first marriage, and, I guess, to start believing in love again. You know, there's always been something between Jonathan and I, but I just pushed it away because I didn't think I could be with a good guy. Who knows? Maybe there are second chances."

"Like me meeting you. That's my second chance already. And I think it's working out. You should totally give Jonathan a chance."

Carrie smiled, "Maybe I will."

Jaz felt a bit like a proud parent when Carrie came downstairs the next evening ready for her date. She had her hair down with soft curls around her face. The green and silver of the dress set off her summer tan, and the dress fit her perfectly. The white strappy heels were perfect, and the completed outfit looked like something from a magazine. It didn't hurt that Carrie couldn't stop smiling. Jaz had a feeling the night would go very well.

When Jonathan came to the door, he was almost speechless. Jaz and

Katie were coloring at the table, so Jaz had a perfect view of his face when he first saw Carrie. She was glad she had told him to dress up. His grey dress shirt, white tie, and dark pants set off Carrie's outfit nicely. They'd definitely be the best-looking couple wherever they were going.

"Isn't Mommy beautiful?" Katie piped up from the kitchen table.

Jonathan cleared his throat. "Is there a word for more than beautiful?"

"Yep! It's beautifuller!"

"Then your mom is beautifuller!"

Carrie waved goodbye and stepped out, and Jaz and Katie shared a giggle. "Do you think Mommy and Uncle Johnny will love each other like in the movies?" Katie wondered.

"Hmmm… normally I'd say no, but I think maybe they will. Your mom's so nice, any guy would be lucky to be with her."

Katie's face fell, "My daddy didn't love her."

Jaz didn't know what to say. Matthew saved the day from his spot on the couch where he was watching a movie. "That's because he was too mad at everything to see how good she was. He'll probably never even know what he missed."

"Uncle Johnny's not mad. He's happy. And silly!"

Eager to change the topic, Jaz asked them about their school. Soon they were both chattering away and Jaz breathed a sigh of relief. She hoped she'd be better at handling tricky topics by the time her baby was old enough to ask questions.

After Katie, and then Matthew went to bed, Jaz made sure they were OK to come to the basement if they needed anything, and then got to work sewing. She had a list going on her phone with all her upcycling ideas for clothes, and she was keen to get started. Already she wanted to branch out and do clothes for everyone —

not just maternity and kids' clothes. And as soon as she knew if she was having a boy or girl she would start styling some baby clothes.

They had made a quick stop at the thrift store again earlier that day. Carrie wanted to get as many frames done as possible before she started school, and Jaz was looking for clothes she could sell. After the two women bought her jean jackets, her followers had jumped up. Jaz suspected it was from word of mouth and them showing off their clothes. She needed to find some things she could easily convert into sales.

Her first project was turning some blouses into maternity wear. A browse on Pinterest had given her some ideas that she thought would be perfect. Taking the first blouse—a light gray short-sleeved cotton blouse—she cut straight up the center of the blouse at the back until she reached the yoke. Then she finished the raw edges, and inserted a triangle of pure white lace cut from a round table-cloth. The last step was to finish the seam at the bottom.

When she looked it over, Jaz thought it was still too prissy. On a whim, she removed the collar and finished the seam. Much better. Now it looked different from the front, but the back was striking with the gray against the white lace.

The other two blouses went much faster, and then she moved on to t-shirts. She had a handful of good-quality, soft men's t-shirts in different colors and a few kids' t-shirts in bright colors. First she altered the large shirts to fit a pregnant woman. It was easy to base it on her own changing body, and then just increase the size for larger women.

After cutting the arms and neck off the bright kids' shirts, she cut the seams so she had rectangles of fabric which she tacked onto the inside front of each of the larger shirts. Then she used a piece of Katie's sidewalk chalk to trace out the words *OH BABY* on the front of each shirt in block letters. After sewing around the letters, she carefully cut out inside each letter, letting the bright background color show through. Then she trimmed the excess fabric from inside the shirt. The finished results was super-soft maternity t-shirts with fun cut-out letters.

Jaz loved the look so much she decided to keep the smallest of the shirts for herself. It was a black t-shirt with camouflage pink letters showing through. While she didn't usually wear pink, she loved the contrast on the black t-shirt. She was vaguely aware of hearing Carrie come in from her date, but was too wrapped up in her projects to go say hi.

CHAPTER 18

When Jaz went upstairs the next morning she wore her new t-shirt with jean shorts that had stretchy panels on each side. She had to admit, this new style was a lot more comfortable than the preppy name-brand clothes she used to live in. Carrie wanted to see everything she had done right away, but Jaz insisted on hearing about her date first.

She blushed and smiled, "It was... perfect." With a little laugh she continued, "I've been fighting this whole falling for him thing since the day I met him. And last night, I finally felt ready to relax my heart a bit. So... there's officially an 'us'." The smile on Carrie's face seemed to light up the whole room.

"Awesome! I think you guys make the best couple!"

"You definitely get some credit for making this happen. I'll have to introduce you to my sister Jessica one day. She'll be very pleased with the progress you've made on me."

Jaz really didn't think she had done much but it was nice to be included in Carrie's happy news. She wished there was *something* she could do to make sure everything would work out for Carrie and Jonathan.

"So," Carrie interrupted her thoughts, "Did I hear the sewing machine still going when I got home last night?"

"Oh, yeah. I got a bunch of things ready to sell. I think I finally realized the other day that I need to start planning for our future — my baby's and mine. And I know I need money to do it. But honestly, I just totally get into the sewing and the time flies. Want to see the stuff?"

"Of course!" Carrie followed Jaz downstairs. Her eyes widened in shock to see the three blouses and five t-shirts Jaz showed her. "Wait, the one you're wearing... that's yours too, isn't it?" Jaz nodded. "Geez, I just assumed you bought it from some hip store I didn't know about. It is *so* cool!"

"The only thing is... I need a model for these ones for taller women, and a photographer for the ones I can fit. Um, would you be able to help me?"

Carrie's face turned serious, and Jaz worried that she had asked too much. After all, she was already living here and using the entire basement.

"On one condition..."

"What? Anything! Anything at all!"

"Will you remember us plain people when you're rich and famous?" Carrie burst out laughing at Jaz's face. "I'm actually kind of serious Jaz. You're going to go far with this!" She hugged Jaz tightly. "I'm blown away by how you're handling this new life of yours."

Jaz relaxed into Carrie and enjoyed the hug before stepping back, "And you don't mind wearing a pillow and looking pregnant? I remade a pillow to look as close to a baby belly as possible..."

"For you Jaz, anything. *After* I have coffee of course."

Carrie suggested they borrow Kara's back yard to take the pictures, since it was landscaped. So that evening they all went over for their first fashion shoot. With Kara's running commentary about Carrie's sudden pregnancy, and the kids laughing at her hamming it up whenever Jaz wanted to take a picture, it was the most fun Jaz remembered having. And when Jonathan joined them, the look on his face when he saw Carrie looking suddenly pregnant had them all gasping for breath in between laughing.

After they finished with the photos, they all sat on the deck after with iced tea, chips, and salsa, enjoying the warm evening. Jaz posted all the pictures while they were visiting, and Carrie and Kara quickly liked and shared them all.

"So, Jaz," Kara started, "Carrie says you're thinking of doing more than maternity clothes?"

"Definitely! I have a ton of ideas for everything from baby stuff and kid's stuff to outfits for seniors. It's so much fun to turn things into new outfits." She beamed at Kara, "And to think, this all started because you took me to Carrie's."

"Don't you forget it!" Kara teased, "You know, if you want to name some hip line of clothes after me or something, feel free."

Jonathan leaned forward, "Well, that does bring up the whole branding thing."

Jaz looked at Jonathan, surprised. She thought he was talking to Ken about football, not listening to them. "What do you mean?"

"Are you going to have a name for your business as a whole? Or for each category separately? And how will you reach the different customers? From what I've seen, people will want to buy your clothes as soon as they see them. You just need to figure out how to be seen by the right people."

"I suppose jazzygurl2.0 isn't the best business name..." Seeing his confused look, she explained, "That's my Instagram handle, and all

I'm using right now to show what I'm selling. But I'm not sure how to change that."

"It's a totally different business than mine, but the idea of finding your ideal customer is the same. I'll send you some blogs that I found really helpful when I was setting up my own business."

"Thanks!" Jaz thought back to her old friends. None of them could offer anything close to the support, advice, and genuine caring that she got from the people around her now. She rubbed her belly and said a silent thank you to the little life that had given her this chance to do something she really loved. All that was missing from the picture was having her parents with her.

CHAPTER 19

*C*arrie and the kids insisted on going with Jaz to Lisa's house when she moved. Lisa offered to drive her, but they put up such a stink that Jaz agreed to let Carrie drive. "But no tears, OK? You're getting your basement back!" She was pretty sure Katie would still cry though.

After loading everything in the car, Carrie came out with her sewing machine. "I won't have any time for sewing for the next eight months, so you can take care of this for me." Jaz thanked her profusely, and they all piled in for the short drive to Lisa's.

When they pulled into the driveway Jaz didn't know whether to laugh or cry. "Seriously? My parent's house is, like, three blocks away."

Carrie turned to look at her carefully, "Are you OK with that?"

Jaz slowly smiled, "Yeah, actually. I am. They can't ignore me for forever."

They all helped bring things in, and Lisa showed Jaz to her room. It was a big bright room with a single bed that had a teal blue comforter on it, a night table with a lamp, and another door that Lisa showed her led into a shared bathroom. "I'll always let you know when another guest is staying here. So far it's been almost all women, and many of them we hardly see. And over here is your studio..." Lisa walked out into the hallway and into another bedroom that faced the front yard. It had a folding table set up with a chair in front of it, as well as a standing lamp and a full-length mirror. "I didn't know what else you needed to get started, but I hope this is OK."

"Are you kidding? This is perfect!" She laughed at the sad faces looking at her, "Hey you three, I'm not that far away. And I'll always remember your basement as the place where it all started."

"Come on down you all. Mom found an amazing bakery nearby and we have donuts for everybody!"

They all trooped back down the stairs and joined Maria at the dining room table. Lisa got drinks for everyone, and they each choose a favorite donut. As soon as the kids finished they asked if they could go play with Becky. "Of course," Maria answered, "I told her mom you might be coming and she said to come down if you wanted. Take your shoes! There's a playhouse in the backyard now."

The kids grabbed their shoes and ran downstairs.

"Who's Becky?" Jaz asked.

"Becky's the daughter of the people who live in the suite downstairs. Their names are Chris and Carla. Wonderful people, and we're lucky to have them living here! Carla helps with the housecleaning so you'll see her around, and Chris does some of the yardwork for me. Becky's Matthew's age, but she's special needs. So I guess mentally she's around three years old, but she doesn't talk. Right now Carla's taken the summer off to be with Becky, but when school starts again, Mom will watch Becky after school every day until Chris or Carla gets home from work."

"Matthew's one of Becky's champions at school," Maria added, "And she loves to play with both kids. She can tell when someone has a good heart."

Jaz listened to the conversation around her, and wondered what it would be like to be around someone who was special needs. She knew that the parents at her high school had worked hard to stop the integration of special needs kids, but she hadn't really thought much about it. Of course someone like Matthew would find a way to be nice to kids like Becky. She hoped Becky would like her, too.

After Carrie and the kids said a sad goodbye, Jaz went upstairs to get her things unpacked. Carrie had given her a few extra-large Ikea bags to put all her projects in, but Jaz still had to put her own growing wardrobe in some grocery bags to bring it all over. The sewing room had a big closet that was already stocked with wooden hangers. It was fun to hang up the things she had for sale. Jaz wondered if it would be OK to invite women up here to shop. That way she could sell more than one thing at a time. At Carrie's she just met them at the door with whatever they had ordered. After the clothes were all hung up, she set up the sewing machine. Already she was thinking of which project to start next…

She went back to set up her own things in her bedroom and sat on the bed to check her Instagram feed before going back down for supper. Someone had messaged her, asking if they could try on one of the maternity dresses upcycled from a man's shirt. It reminded her of the times when clients would come to her grandma's to try on clothes.

The smell of stir-fry convinced her it was time to head downstairs. Lisa had insisted she eat meals with them, "I'm guessing you hardly eat, so it's not like it makes a difference to the budget. But we like it better when there's more people at the table."

"I'm not sure if you're used to real Chinese food, but I do a decent stir-fry… I think." Lisa was setting the table, and Maria was already sitting down. She motioned to an empty chair for Jaz.

"Oh, um, do you want me to help with anything before I sit down?"

"No, that's OK. Thanks though."

Over dinner Lisa and Maria asked Jaz a lot of questions about her business, her projects, and her pregnancy. Eventually the conversation veered to her parents.

"You won't believe this, but they live just a few blocks from here. I've walked past your house a ton of times in the past!"

"How do you feel, being closer to them?"

"Carrie asked me the same thing. It's OK. I mean, obviously they're still super mad at me, and don't want me in their life. But I miss them. I wish I could tell them that I'm OK, and that they can still be proud of me."

Lisa and Maria exchanged looks. It was Maria who spoke up first, "You know, Jaz. I wasn't a very good mom when Lisa was little. My husband scared me, and I thought the best way to deal with him was to keep my distance from Lisa. When I look back now, I can see how terribly hurtful I was to Lisa. I didn't even go to her graduation because Robert said we weren't going."

Jaz couldn't help but gasp. How could they be so happy together now? It couldn't have been that long ago that Lisa graduated.

Lisa took over the story, "That day that I graduated, I left home without ever planning on coming back. I was convinced there was nothing for me at home, and I was determined to make my own good life. And I did! I rented a room, got a couple jobs, and ended up going to college to become a bookkeeper. I had a friend that encouraged me to keep in contact with Mom, but that only meant I called her once a year on her birthday. Then my dad suddenly died, and my mom was left with nothing."

"It was really like less than nothing," Maria added. "For my whole adult, life Robert had controlled every single thing. I couldn't make the simplest decision on my own. And my health was deteriorating so much I couldn't take care of myself."

"Lisa came home for the funeral, and took care of everything. When she found out that I really had nothing, she put her life on hold for me. She moved me here to the city, and helped me gain the confidence to start living again. I'm so grateful she forgave me for all my mistakes, and she gave our relationship a second chance. Never give up hope Jaz. Your parents will come around!"

Jaz felt tears fill her eyes. That was what she desperately wanted, but after a whole summer of not hearing from them, she *had* given up hope. "Thanks. I think... your story... it's so sad, and then so beautiful."

Jaz stayed in the kitchen to help Lisa clean up supper. She was glad her time at Carrie's had taught her how to do things like wash pots and pans and load the dishwasher. "Where did your mom go?" She asked, when she realized Maria wasn't at the table anymore.

"She's probably in bed already. I'll check on her after we're done. She has rheumatoid arthritis. Have you hear of it?"

"Yeah, that's an autoimmune disease, right?"

"Right. She's been doing really well, but she tires really easily. And when she has flares—that's when the symptoms go crazy on her—then she pretty much stays in bed and toughs it out until it goes into remission."

"Wow, that's terrible. Isn't there anything they can do?"

"Well, she's on better pain meds, and she takes these pills that suppress her immune system, which helps control the flares. But it also means she gets sick a lot easier. I've heard there's some alternative treatments that might help, but she's not ready to try anything new yet."

Jaz wished she could make Maria better. She almost said so, but Lisa continued talking. "So, I'm usually out the door by eight for work in the morning. There's coffee, tea, and breakfast things in the cupboard here. Mom is up by ten. If she's not up by then, please check on her. And if you have any concerns don't hesitate to send me a text. OK?"

"Um, yeah, sure! And thank you so much for letting me stay here."

Lisa turned and leaned her back against the sink, "You're welcome! I'm really happy to have you—Mom is too. I'm going to watch some TV for a bit now. You're welcome to join me. Although it's pretty much guaranteed to be a home reno show. I don't know if that's your thing."

"Actually, I kinda want to work on some clothes if that's OK?"

"It's only OK if you promise to never ask if it's OK again! You're in charge of your life here."

Jaz smiled, "You sound just like Carrie."

"Where do you think I got it from?" With a smirk Lisa went into the living room.

Up in her new sewing room, Jaz realized she hadn't asked about letting women in to try on clothes. She reluctantly went back downstairs, wishing she didn't have to bother Lisa.

"So, um, Lisa? I know you said not to ask… but this is a bit different. I had someone ask if they could try things on before buying them. Is that OK? If people come in? I don't think it would be very often.."

"Are you kidding? More people coming in and out? You'll be Mom's best friend in no time, she'd love it!"

Jaz let out the breath she didn't realize she was holding, "Really? I mean, that's great, thank you!"

"As long as you don't mind Mom making friends with all your clients, too. She's the biggest social butterfly I've ever met. And on her good days she'd be more than happy to let people in."

"Cool, and thanks!"

Jaz ran upstairs, feeling excited. She could almost run a real business like her ma ma had, having people over, getting them into clothes they loved. Her mind started spinning with all the possibilities.

CHAPTER 20

"Good morning Jaz!" Maria was sitting at the table with a mug in front of her. She wore a bright floral robe, and her bare feet showed purple toenails. Her short hair was stylishly swept to the side.

"Oh, hi Maria!" Jaz went in the kitchen where the kettle still had hot water. She made a cup of tea and joined Maria.

"How are you feeling?"

"Me, I'm fine? How about you? Lisa was telling me a bit about your arthritis last night."

"It's a good day today. But I'm not the one who's pregnant!"

"Oh, that. Yeah, I think the morning sickness is finally over." Jaz took a sip of her tea. She wondered what Carrie and the kids were doing for a minute before trying to focus on her new living situation. "So, I might have one or two people coming to try on some clothes. I asked Lisa last night and she said it was OK…"

"Sounds fun! I'd love to see everything you're doing. I always wanted to learn to make my own clothes. And I can let people in for you!"

"Lisa did say you liked to have people over."

"Love it! The more people the better!"

Jaz made herself a piece of toast, and Maria left to get dressed. When she came back she was wearing a bright yellow t-shirt, tan capris, and short socks with white runners.

"Wow! That's a bright t-shirt!"

"I insist on only wearing bright colors. For so many years I dressed like an old lady—plain blouses and polyester pants. When Lisa took me to the mall for the first time I was totally lost! But we figured it out. The only thing is finding things I can get on and off myself. Sometimes these joints don't like moving! But, like I said, today's a good day so I could wear a proper t-shirt." She took her own toast out of the toaster and added butter and honey before joining Jaz at the table. "But enough about me! Tell me about the clothes you're making and the people that buy them."

"Well, everything I'm selling is used, which is kinda funny, because the people who buy my clothes wouldn't be caught dead in a thrift store. I started with maternity clothes that are unique and *not* cute or too girly. Everything I've done so far is selling. But last week I did a bunch of clothes for Matthew and Katie and it was *so* much fun! So now I think I'll do clothes for everyone." Her eyes twinkled, "And I did a dress for Carrie and made her wear it on a date with Jonathan, and now they're officially dating!"

"That's wonderful! I was watching them at Carrie's barbeque and they seemed to be so perfectly matched. I do hope things work out for them. And how do people find your clothes?"

"Instagram! These ladies came up to me in the mall a few weeks ago because they liked the maternity jacket I was wearing. Carrie got them to start following me on Instagram, and it's kinda gone crazy from there."

"Can you show me that? I've never been on Instagram. Here, let me get my laptop."

Jaz spent the next twenty minutes explaining Instagram to Maria, and showing her how she posted things for sale. "This is funny. When I first got to Carrie's, she showed me how her website worked and everything, and now I'm here showing you the same things for my stuff!"

"I really love how the internet lets you all connect and sell your things. It's absolutely genius! Now, how can I help you?"

Jaz was speechless. Help? She had no right to ask this lady with an autoimmune disease to help her!

"Honestly Jaz. I have a lot of time on my hands, and I'd rather be busy. I do all the Airbnb stuff for Lisa and I love it, but it doesn't exactly take up my days!"

"Um, I don't really know. Well, just having you OK with people coming over to try things on, that's helpful…" Jaz had spent so much mental energy focusing on doing everything herself for her and her baby that she had trouble thinking about *not* doing it all herself.

"How about you start by showing me some clothes? I can make it up the stairs today."

With that, Jaz welcomed Maria into her world. She proudly showed her everything she had for sale—the maternity dresses from men's shirts, the t-shirts with cut-outs, and the one jean jacket she still had available. Then she went through the clothes waiting for work, sharing her ideas.

"And how much will people pay for these clothes?"

"Well, so far I've been selling the jean jackets for $95, the dresses for $70, and the t-shirts for $45. If I work all day and sell what I've done I can make about $150 a day or more…" Jaz had never talked to anyone about money. Her parents always treated their income as secret, and she didn't know why she was talking to Maria about it now.

"Oh, that makes me so happy! It's so important that you have your own income that you're in control of. You know, part of the reason I felt so trapped with Robert was that I had no way of making money. Sometimes I wonder how many women are in the same situation."

"Really? I mean, I've never thought about it. I know people talk about women going back to bad relationships, or not leaving even though they should. It seems wrong that money—or I guess, not having money—would trap them."

"I agree, it *is* wrong." Maria ran her hand over the sweatpants Jaz had left out on the sewing table. "What on earth can you do with this? Sure, the fabric is incredibly soft... but ugh."

"Well, I'm not sure it will work yet. But I want to turn it into a sporty skirt. Maybe not maternity, but for someone like Lisa or Carrie. There's enough fabric here to make the skirt, and I can even re-use the elastic from the waistband. Then I want to use this red seam binding to run two stripes up each side. It's amazing how often you can find brand new sewing supplies in the baskets at the thrift store."

"So it's just a comfortable pull-on skirt?"

"Yeah. What do you think?"

"I think you're a genius! Now, if you're going to have women coming up here to try things on, we have to do something about this room. I wonder if Chad could install a three-way mirror against the wall there... And definitely a comfy chair for people to sit on, especially if you have pregnant women trying on clothes... And the walls. They could use a set of Carrie's frames! I'm going to go look on that Buy and Sell site to see what I can find. What look do you want? Colorful? Or black and white?"

"Well, I think I'm more of a black and white person. So maybe something monochromatic? Then the clothes can be the color."

"Perfect! I'll leave you to your sewing then." And with that Maria left.

After cutting off the seams from the sweatpants, Jaz got out the sidewalk chalk that Katie insisted she keep and started sketching a rough pattern for the skirt. The pants were an extra-large, and she soon realized there was enough fabric to make a matching skirt in a child's size. With a quick check on her phone where she kept a list of Carrie, Matthew, and Katie's measurements, she got to work.

When her stomach told her it was lunchtime, Jaz gathered both finished skirts to bring down and show Maria. Walking into the living room where Maria was watching TV, she held up both skirts. "What do you think?"

"Oh my goodness. Those are beyond cute! Wow!"

"Thanks! I'm going to go back to the thrift stores this afternoon and see how many more pairs of sweatpants I can find. Then maybe Carrie and Katie will come over for a photo shoot, and I can give them a set as a thank you."

"I can't wait to see them on your site! Lisa made two containers of stir-fry for us to have for lunch. Is that OK with you?"

"Yep, can I heat yours up for you?"

"That would be nice, thank you." Maria turned off the TV and came to sit at the table while Jaz got lunch ready for the two of them. She felt so grown-up making lunch for another adult. Well, she wasn't actually *making* it, but she was serving someone! She wished she had done something like this for her mom when she had the chance.

Her phone pinging interrupted her thoughts. "Oh! It looks like a lady wants to try things on tomorrow morning. Fortunately she's a size medium, so I should have some different things for her. She's only looking for a dress, but I want to try and get more sold."

They both started eating, and Maria smiled at Jaz, "Did you always know you had good business sense?"

"Um, no. Not at all! But I guess I learned a lot watching my ma ma —that's grandma. I remember one time this guy came in for her to fix the zipper on his jacket, and by the time he left she had convinced him to get all his pants hemmed, and his suit jacket tailored. She could see how to help people look their best, and then she always convinced them to hire her for it!"

"You're so lucky you had that time with her."

Jaz agreed. The rest of lunch she talked about how she always listened to Jaz, even when she was working, and how her favorite times where when she had to stay at ma ma's for supper and she'd get her undivided attention. After cleaning up from lunch she asked if Maria wanted to go with her to the thrift stores.

"Oh, that would be so fun, but I'm afraid I'm not up to the busses and walking. You'll have to show me everything when you come home!"

As she headed out to the bus stop, Jaz looked at the car in the drive-way. She *did* have her license... And it looked like Lisa didn't need the car during the daytime. Jaz felt bad for Maria stuck at home every day. Maybe when she could pay Lisa rent, she'd ask if she could use the car, too.

On the bus Jaz took out her phone and did some calculations. If she could sell $200 of clothes every day, she could pay Lisa rent and start saving for baby things. She wondered how much rent would be. $1000? More? Less? With a sigh, Jaz had to acknowledge that there was still a lot of life stuff she knew nothing about.

That night, over a dinner of chicken Caesar salad, Jaz asked about some of the things that she had been thinking about.

"How did you figure out how to do everything when you left home? I mean, all the adult stuff." she asked Lisa.

"Well, when I was still in high school I had one teacher who under-stood the situation with my dad, and kind of became my mentor. He helped me make a resume so I could get a job, and told me where to get a bank account, and how to get my own cell phone contract. Then, before I graduated I did a lot of research into rent and jobs in the city."

"It was still a huge shock when I got here. Then I had to ask lots of people for help. The lady at the bank helped me switch to an adult account, and the seniors at the bus stop helped me figure out public transportation. Oh, and my roommate at the time dragged me all over the city to movies, concerts, restaurants, and malls. That might not seem like a big deal, but for this country bumpkin it was an important education."

"Wow. You're so brave! I don't know what I would have done without Kara and Carrie to help me out when my parents kicked me out."

"But that's just the thing," Maria pointed out. "You found the right people to help you, and you accepted their help. So in your own way, you figured things out too!"

"I guess so… But there's still so much I don't know. Like, um, how much should I plan to pay for rent? And are there other things I need to pay for?"

"Amy paid $600 per month for the bedroom, so how about $700 per month for both rooms? Only when you're making good sales, though. I don't want you pinching pennies!"

"Actually, I think I can pay you that pretty soon! I already sold a couple hundred dollars of stuff at Carrie's. And I have a lady coming tomorrow to try things on. I think it's like Carrie's business. The most I post, the more things sell."

"That's fantastic! How are you keeping track of everything?" Lisa gestured at the salad, and Jaz gladly took another portion.

"Well, I get paid either in cash or from PayPal. And then I just… spend it?"

Lisa grinned, "You know I'm a bookkeeper, right?" Jaz nodded. "And I love setting up accounts and tracking for people…"

"But you've already done so much to help me!"

Lisa rolled her eyes, "And?"

"Well, I just, couldn't ask you for more help!"

"Great! I'll just insist on helping you and then you won't have to ask!"

Maria laughed, "Give up Jaz. She's going to help you whether you ask or not!"

They all cleaned up supper, and then Jaz brought down her laptop and sat beside Lisa. An hour later she had a basic accounting program installed that would help her keep track of her expenses and income.

"This is really important because you'll always know how your business is doing. And when it comes time for taxes, it's just a matter of submitting your numbers."

"I have to pay taxes?" Jaz hadn't thought about anything like that.

"No, you *get* to pay taxes. This is a bit of a thing for me. I really believe that our taxes are used in part to help our friends and neighbors. After all, without taxes who would pay for our schools, roads, security, and a ton of other things? So I'm always happy to pay my taxes. One, because it's going to many of the things that make this a great place to live, and two, because I'm actually earning enough to have to pay taxes!"

"OK…I guess you're right. Um, thanks for helping me set this all up. I actually feel better having this here to show me how I'm doing. I've never had to budget, or plan, or do any of that stuff and I want to be good at it before I have my baby."

"Good for you! I think by the time your little one comes along you'll be set!"

They were interrupted by a knock at the door leading to the downstairs suite. "Come in!" Maria called.

First through the door was a slight girl with wispy blond hair. Seeing Jaz, she stopped suddenly and the man behind her had to gently push her forward before stepping up into the room.

"Becky, this is our friend Jaz. Jaz, meet Becky." Jaz was surprised that Lisa talked to her like she'd talk to Matthew or Katie. She was about to say hello, but found Becky's direct gaze a little disconcerting.

Becky walked slowly over to Jaz, reached up, and gently took her hair in her hand. The guy behind her walked over and stood beside Jaz, facing Becky. "Her hair is special, isn't it Becky?"

Becky's gaze turned to him before she turned back to Jaz. Letting go of her hair, she took Jaz's hand in both of hers before leaning against Jaz's side.

"Um, hi Becky…" She didn't know what to do, but she didn't want to scare Becky or upset her.

"And I'm Chris, Becky's dad."

Jaz looked up at him and smiled.

"What are you two up to?"

"Oh, Jaz and I have been setting up an accounting system for her business." Lisa answered. "Good timing, we just finished."

"Ah, so I'm in the presence of creative greatness. Maria told me all about Jaz and her business. Becky, you stay here while I go get the stuff from the truck." He turned and went out the front door leaving Jaz wondering what to do next.

"Becky," Lisa said gently, "Maybe you could go get a cookie, and then sit beside Jaz instead of standing on top of her."

Becky reluctantly let go of Jaz's hand before going to the cupboard and getting a cookie. She carefully moved a chair right against Jaz before sitting down beside her.

"Oh, I see you've made friends already!" Maria walked into the room and went over to hug Becky and kiss her cheek. Becky wiped her face and glared at her. "I'll kiss the other cheek too little missy, just you wait!" A giggle burst from the little girl and Jaz realized they were both teasing. Maria continued a one-sided conversation with Becky, asking about her day and what she had for supper while using what looked like basic sign language.

When Chris came back in he was carrying some large panels which he put down and went back out for more supplies.

"I asked Chris to make a proper mirror for your room upstairs," Maria explained. "He's a contractor so he'll do a good job!"

"Oh, wow. That's fast!"

"Did you want to show me where you want it?" he asked, coming back in the door with a handful of metal parts. Jaz followed him upstairs, and realized he was going to build her a three-way mirror that could fold closed when she needed more space in the room.

"Are you serious? This is like a real professional mirror! Amazing! How much do I owe you for it?" The words popped out of Jaz's mouth before she realized that she probably didn't have enough money to pay him. Maybe she could do part now, and part next week—

"No cost. This came from a store I'm remodeling right now. It was perfect timing that Maria called today, because they would have been in the dumpster by tomorrow morning. All I had to do was take the hardware down and bring it home. So, if this is where you want it I'll get to work and then call you up when it's finished."

"OK... thank you so much! Can I make some clothes for Becky or your wife as a thank you?"

"Oh! Well... Becky's pretty picky about her clothes. You'd have to ask Carla about that because I always forget what stuff she won't wear. But Carla... I don't know what she likes. If you could figure that out, I'd be impressed!"

"Can I go look in her closet?" Jaz shocked herself by asking such a bold question.

"What? Well yeah, I guess so. She's working an evening shift at the store so she won't be home until ten or so. Down the stairs, through the living room, second door."

Jaz left him to his work and went into the basement. She was amazed at what she found—or rather what she *didn't* find. Carla had even fewer clothes than Carrie! All her life Jaz had assumed that women shopped and bought clothes they only wore once or twice. That was what her mom and all her friends did. But the women she was meeting now were different. Either they didn't like clothes as much—which Jaz didn't believe for a second—or they *couldn't* buy clothes.

She learned a few things about Carla from her clothes. One, that she was about the same size as Carrie. Two, she must be cold all the time, because almost every shirt was long-sleeved. Three, everything she owned was really worn out. But with so few clothes Jaz really couldn't figure out what style Carla might like. She smiled to herself. This would be fun!

CHAPTER 21

The next week Jaz sold clothes every day, and worked on projects late into the night. She was feeling confident and successful until she realized it was the week she was supposed to start university. After seeing out her last client of the day she put on a pair of runners and her jean jacket over a t-shirt and shorts and went for a walk.

Finding herself at her parent's house, she crossed the street and sat on the sidewalk, leaning back against a streetlight pole. It didn't look like anything had changed. The house still had a perfectly manicured lawn with carefully trimmed hedges on either side of the front door. The curtains were pulled back at exactly the right angle, and the windows were spotless. All that was different was Jaz. Had she changed too much to ever be able to come home?

The neighbor pulled into the driveway and got out of his car wearing a suit and carrying a briefcase. He gave Jaz a strange look and then walked into the house. Minutes later a police car pulled up and parked beside her. A police officer got out and walked over to Jaz.

"You got any ID on you?"

"Yeah, um…" Suddenly all the stories Jaz heard about profiling ran through her head. Was she in trouble? Did the neighbor call the police on her? "It's just in my purse here. Can I stand up first?"

"Yes, slowly." He stood above her with his hands on his hips.

"No problem there…" she mumbled as she slowly stood up. Her legs were stiff from sitting on the pavement. Once standing, she opened the small purse she always wore over her shoulder and pulled out her driver's license.

He looked at it carefully and then turned until he saw her house number. "Wait, you live here?"

"Yes. No. Sort of. That's my home, but my parents made me leave when they found out I was pregnant. I just came by to see if they're OK…" Jaz was horrified to feel tears filling her eyes.

"If you live here, why do the neighbors think you're here to cause trouble?"

Jaz sighed, "I look different. Nobody recognizes me anymore. And my parents told everyone I left for a gap year in Europe."

"Well, you can't loiter in neighborhoods like this, even if it's your parent's house. And you need ID with your current address if you don't live here anymore." He pulled out his notebook and wrote something down from her driver's license before handing it back to her.

"OK, I'm going." Jaz made her way back down the street. She took a quick look at the neighbor's window and saw him standing to the side, watching her. Turning around, she could also see the police officer still standing there with his hands on his hips. Three months ago she probably would have been suspicious if someone looking like her was hanging around the house. Strange how quickly things could change.

Maria was sitting on the couch watching TV when she came in the door. "Jaz? Is that you?"

"Yeah," she took off her runners and walked into the living room.

"What is it? Come here! You don't look so good." Maria patted the spot beside her on the couch and Jaz sat down and told her what had happened. This time the tears started and didn't stop. Maria wrapped her arm around her, and Jaz cried out all the hurt, pain, and rejection. When she quieted down, Maria kissed her cheek, just like she would kiss Becky's. "You listen to me. You are a kind, sweet, smart, creative young lady, and you are a gift to everyone who's lucky enough to spend time with you. Don't forget that! I can only imagine how much it hurt to be treated like that, but don't hang on to it. You're surrounded by people here who know how wonderful you are. And one day, your mom and dad will be part of that."

Jaz sniffed, "Thanks," she whispered. There was something so comforting about being held in a mom's arms. She took a shuddering breath and closed her eyes...

The sound of quiet conversation wafted into Jaz's ears. Slowly she realized she was sleeping with her head in Maria's lap, and Maria was gently stroking her hair. "Hello Jazzy girl. Take your time. I'm not going anywhere."

"Oh, wow." She sat up, and looked across at Lisa who was sitting in an armchair with her legs tucked underneath her. "I, um... how long was I asleep?"

"Not too long. Maybe 45 minutes. I think all your late nights' sewing, and the stress of today knocked you out. I told Lisa what happened."

"I'm so sorry Jaz," Lisa's voice was gentle. "I can't even imagine what that was like. Mom and I thought you deserved to have some comfort food tonight but we don't know what you like. Any ideas?"

Jaz thought for a minute. "Yeah, actually... but you won't like it."

"Try me," Maria challenged.

"Can we go to McDonald's? I know it's lame, but I'm totally craving it!"

Half an hour later they were sitting in McDonald's eating supper. It was the perfect thing to help Jaz feel better, and afterwards she went straight to bed and slept for ten hours.

Over the next few months, Jaz and Maria became almost insepara-ble. Maria gave Jaz the love and care that she was craving, and Jaz included Maria in almost everything she did. They joked about their strange partnership, but everyone around them could see how well it worked.

Jaz gave Maria full access to her Instagram and messaging, and Maria took over booking women to try on clothes, letting them in and out of the house, and generally making every one of them feel like they were special clients. With Maria taking care of all the logis-tics of the business, and Lisa helping her track her sales and expenses, Jaz could completely get lost for hours in her sewing room.

As Jaz's body continued to change and she wondered if she would be a good mom, or whether her parents would ever forgive her, her creative times sewing gave her a much-needed escape.

Lisa and Maria worried about the hours Jaz spent working, espe-cially when she was up until the early hours of the morning. They noticed how driven she was, and how easy it was for her to set an impossible standard and then try to meet it. The solution came from a very unexpected source.

As Jaz's clients began to have their babies, they asked for more baby and toddler clothes. Many of them felt like their unique style was part of their identity, and they wanted their children to match. So, Jaz started to add a 'baby line'. Her first project was some baby bibs that looked like bandanas. It was easy enough to find unique patterns on clothes at the thrift store—all she had to look for was the right absorbent material. And when she found a bag of vintage iron-on patches to add to the baby bandanas she could hardly keep up with demand.

At the same time, she got ideas for making toddler scarves from t-shirts and baby leg warmers from old sweaters that were also a huge hit. Often when someone came to buy one thing, they walked out the door with entire outfits for their kids. Without Jaz knowing, Maria decided she needed a few days break from seeing clients, and scheduled visits accordingly. The break gave Jaz time to turn all the extra fabric that was piling up into adorable toddler versions of some of the women's clothes she had already sold. There were little sport skirts, t-shirts with heart cut-outs and bright backings, and some soft t-shirt dresses with matching underpants. Now all she needed was someone to model them…

She decided to text Lauren:

> *Hey, this is Jaz. Long time no text! Can I borrow Brittany? I need a model for some toddler outfits. I'll pay you in clothes!*

Lauren immediately replied:

> *babe! thot u forgot me. ya, brit's good to model. need address & time.*

When they arrived the next day, Maria, Jaz, Lauren, and Brittany all trooped downstairs to Chris and Carla's suite. They were borrowing it to change Brittany into the different outfits because it led right out to the backyard so they could take pictures outside. Lisa's backyard was lush and green, and there was a playhouse that made a perfect backdrop if they could get Brittany to use it.

Jaz had also made some coordinating wrap headbands, but after the first outfit Brittany refused to keep one on. It didn't really matter though. Every look was cuter than the last one and Jaz knew she would sell out fast. In less than an hour they had enough pictures of all the outfits, and Maria insisted they all go back upstairs for tea and cake. She had ordered a special cake from the bakery just for Lauren and Brittany's visit.

"So," Lauren started after they were all settled at the table, "How's this whole clothes thing goin'?"

"Way better than I thought! It only takes me about fifteen new followers to have a real client that will buy from me a bunch of times. And that's pretty good, especially since some of the people following me don't live here."

"What are you gonna do when the little squirt comes?"

Jaz was confused, "The same thing?"

Lauren reached over and patted her on the shoulder, "Aw, you're still in 'no baby' land where you have time and energy. Listen, you gotta find a way to keep pushing out the stuff without doin' so much yourself. It's the same thing Carrie had me do for her when she was doin' school and still needed to keep her business goin'"

"Yes!" Maria practically shouted, "Thank you Lauren! Lisa and I keep trying to tell her that, but she keeps on doing it all herself. She works way too hard, even now."

"OK, tell me this. What stuff could someone else do?"

"Um…" Jaz had to think for a minute, "I guess lots of it, if they had some basic sewing skills. Especially this toddler line. The scarves, headbands, and dresses are really simple. Actually, the t-shirts are too. And for the maternity stuff, it's not too hard to alter clothes if you know what you're doing. Again, the t-shirts are easy. Well, I guess the only thing is the jean jackets. Those are pretty complicated. And upselling when clients come."

"What's that?"

"It's when a lady comes for one thing, and I show her other things and get her to buy more. I kind of have a contest with myself to see how well I can figure out what they like and sell it to them."

"That's definitely one of your talents, Jaz." Maria turned to Lauren. "Carla, from downstairs had a really, *really* worn out wardrobe. After looking it over, and talking to us, Jaz figured out that Carla loved classic styles and neutral colors, and she did, like six or seven pieces in total that were just amazing. Even now, when Chris and Carla go out, she looks so confident in her new outfits. She told me she feels like a better person when she's wearing your clothes Jaz!"

"Wow, I had no idea it was that big of a deal! It makes me want to do some more things for her. She works so hard, plus having Becky. It can't be easy."

"The whole mom thing is crazy hard babe. That's why you need to farm some of this work out! Who do you know that can sew?"

"Honestly? No one." Part of Jaz felt excited about the idea of getting some help. If she could get someone else to do more of the sewing, she could see more of her ideas come to life. But there was another part of her that felt sure no one could do what she did.

"Well, I might be able to help…" Maria picked up her phone and started texting. "There! I've sent off a group message to some ladies I met at the library. They're all mostly homebodies who wished they had more things to do. Some of them are older, but not all of them. I'll bet there are a few who know how to sew and would be delighted to have a little bit of work to keep them busy and earn some money." She smiled at Jaz, "I'll keep you in the loop!"

"Great! Now you've pretty much committed me!" Jaz tried unsuccessfully to look upset. She'd do almost anything to make Maria happy—even finally agree to get help.

"I know!" Maria giggled, "Otherwise you'd keep trying to do it all yourself! Now this has been fun, but I'm afraid I need to lie down for a bit." She said goodbye to Lauren and Brittany and then left the room.

Jaz sent all the photos to Lauren before getting her to choose an outfit for Brittany. She choose a grey sporty skirt with pink stripes down the side, a pink t-shirt with a heart cut out and a grey backing, and a pink and gray infinity scarf. "She may ditch the scarf pretty quick but it's the cutest outfit! Dustin's gonna freak when he sees it."

"How's he doing?"

Lauren sighed, "I'm worried. Sometimes I can see in his eyes he'd do almost anything for a high. It never goes away for addicts you know. The craving."

"I didn't—I don't really know anything about that. Isn't there anything you can do? Therapy or something?"

"I dunno. Everyone I know who tries to kick it ends up failing. I know he doesn't want to hurt me. Or Brittany. But sometimes..." She put her face in her hands and rubbed hard before looking up again. "Hey, what am I whining about? I got a gorgeous kid, and a dude who loves me, and I get to make art for a living. I'm good!"

Jaz wished there was something she could do to help Lauren. In her old life she never would have spent time with anyone who did drugs —or knew someone who did drugs. She cringed at all the jokes she and her friends used to make about the druggies begging downtown. Now that she was around different people, her views were definitely changing.

CHAPTER 22

The huge increase in sales when Jaz started posting the toddler outfits convinced her to get all the help she could. Maria found three ladies who all said they could sew, and set up appointments for each of them to visit Jaz.

She could tell pretty quickly what skill level each of them was at, and started getting ideas for which projects each might do before they were even out the door. Lisa helped her set up simple contracts with set prices for each item they completed. Jaz liked the idea of leaving it up to each person how much/little they wanted to do, and paying them for each individual project. Even with paying them a decent rate, Lisa showed Jaz that she was still making an average of 60% profit on each sale.

Maria had the inside scoop on each of the ladies' situations, and she knew that two of them would probably quickly complete everything Jaz could throw at them. "What do you think of paying them every Friday? I know for some of them, having that extra money every week would really help."

"Oh," Jaz's face fell, "That sounds like a lot of work. I hadn't thought about how to pay them…"

"It's another chance for you to ask for help," Lisa reminded her. "What if you had Mom handle all the administrative stuff with your contractors? She'll be great at keeping them in line. I know you're already paying her to help with all the bookings and stuff."

Jaz loved being able to pay Maria to help her out. And she loved the idea of having more help and less work at the same time. "Done! That is, if you want the job?" She smirked at Maria, knowing she couldn't stop her if she tried.

"Oh, this is just perfect. Of course I want the job! And I need a title too. What about Personal Assistant to Jasmine Lee? Or maybe Executive Secretary… I like the ring of that!"

"Executive Secretary it is!" Jaz declared, "Along with second mom, wonderful friend, life saver, and great hugger!"

"Gosh, if you weren't pregnant, I'd suggest popping a bottle of prosecco to celebrate! As it is… I guess cups of tea all around!" Lisa got up to put the kettle on to boil, and Jaz made lists of everything she wanted the ladies to do.

"Maria, can you set up meetings for each of them to come back? I have enough stock to get them all started on their first week, so as soon as they're able to come they can get started. Lisa? Can your mom do the contract signing and everything?"

"You need to be there too, but yeah, Mom can be in charge of it. As long as it's your signature. You know Jaz, I think the way things are going you should consider incorporating the business. Why don't you do some research about it? You'll need a lawyer to set everything up, I think. But now that you're hiring contractors it'd be a smart move. Maybe I should have thought of this earlier."

"If it wasn't for you I wouldn't even know how much I was making, so I guess I'll forgive you," Jaz joked. "I still can't believe we had a $1,200 week!" The ladies had all checked the numbers twice, but the reality of such a successful week was slowly sinking in. Jaz promised to do some research into having an incorporated business, and after an hour she knew it was the right step to take. But she wished her dad were around to give her advice. He had been in the business world his whole adult life.

The next day Jaz met with each of the ladies, signed contracts, and sent them home with their first batch of projects. She was starting fairly simple with each of them the first week, but hoped they'd show they could handle a lot more. After they left she had just enough time to head to the thrift stores before they closed. In the past she restricted herself to buying what she thought she could finish in a few weeks. Now, with help available she had fun letting her imagination run wild.

As Maria predicted, the end of the week brought Jaz a slew of finished products. She happily approved all of them so Maria could pay their workers. One older lady quietly asked if she could get paid in cash. Jaz wasn't sure, but Maria whispered to 'just do it' so she went and got cash from the safe where she kept change. Some of her clients did pay in cash, and Jaz had learned to keep enough cash to be able to give change for anything up to $100.

Lisa came home from work with some smokies and a salad she picked up downtown, and went out to start the barbeque before changing out of her work clothes. "That feels better!" she sighed as she slipped on a pair of sandals.

Jaz joined her on the deck while she cooked the smokies. "I wish I knew how to make comfortable dress shoes! Those heels looked painful!"

"You and me both! How did today go?"

"Good! The ladies all brought back their finished work and it looks great. I'll be busy tomorrow posting everything. And we paid them, but one lady asked for cash. So I guess I'll have to keep more cash handy?"

"That's different. But yeah, I guess you should be prepared for that on Friday's then."

"Anything interesting happen at your work today?" Jaz knew that

Lisa often found her job boring. After working two full-time jobs while taking college courses, Lisa was used to being much busier. Now that she had sorted out the accounting department she was in charge of, most of her days were routine — and long.

"Nope. Everything's running smoothly. Seriously, if it wasn't for the freelance work I do in the evenings I'd be bashing my head against my desk. If Carrie wasn't so busy studying, I'd go visit her and get her help to talk things out. I'm starting to dread going to work, just because it's so routine every day."

"Yeah, when I was at Carrie's on Wednesday I pretty much just hung out with Matthew and Katie while she worked on a paper. She looked super tired too." Jaz was keeping her promise to visit every week, and quickly realized that Lauren wasn't kidding when she talked about losing Carrie to her studies.

Back inside with dinner, Maria brought up the lady they paid cash to. "I don't know her full story, but I think she's in a bad situation. From what I've figured out listening to others, women who want to be paid in cash are either trying to have some extra shopping money that can't be tracked, or they're tucking it away for some sort of escape. And she's not the shopping type…"

"You think she's trying to leave her husband?"

"She's not married. She lives with her daughter and grandkids, so I don't really know what's up. And she seems really nice. I just get the feeling something's not right."

"Oh," Jaz helped herself to another smokie. "Well, I hope the sewing helps, whatever's going on."

"It will," Maria said confidently, "You have no idea how empowering it can be for a woman to be in control of earning some money. I think you're going to help change people's lives Jaz."

CHAPTER 23

On the day Jaz incorporated her business she took Lisa and Maria out for dinner to celebrate.

"I can hardly believe I'm a real businesswoman now!"

"Oh, you've been one for a while now. It's just that now you're official. I'm so proud of you!"

"Thanks Maria. I couldn't have done it without your help!" She looked into her messenger bag at the paperwork peeking out. The official name was Jazzy Clothing Company Inc, but she was keeping her Instagram handle as jazzygurl2.0 and just adding her company name to the profile.

"And when you have your business bank account set-up tomorrow you'll be even more official!"

"Again, couldn't have done it without *you*!" She smiled at Lisa and then at Maria before turning to the menu. "This is a celebration, and since I'm driving you should both order a drink or two."

Lisa and Maria exchanged a glance before turning to their wine menus. The changes in Jaz were really amazing. As her baby grew and her body changed she become more confident, and even a little outspoken sometimes. They knew Jaz was headed towards big things, and it was exciting to be a part of her transformation.

Jaz entered the third trimester of her pregnancy and the Christmas season with excitement—and worries. With Maria's encouragement she designed all sorts of dress clothes for everyone from babies to men. They had a hilarious photo shoot with Chris and Carla at the beginning of December so she could post everything.

Jaz used the same technique she started in the summer with Matthew's dress shirt to spice up an entire line of men's dress shirts, and did some coordinating women's wrap dresses with hints of sparkle that were perfect for the holidays.

For Becky, Jaz found a pair of white leggings similar to the type Becky always wore, and added a soft green chiffon skirt to it. She knew that Becky didn't like wearing dresses, but Carla really wanted her to have one dressier outfit for Christmas. Along with a white long-sleeved t-shirt with a Christmas tree cut-out, it was a perfect outfit that Becky was happy to wear. Jaz added making more clothes for kids like Becky to her growing list of ideas. It seemed like no matter how much help she got, she still had more ideas than time.

She thought about her parents every day, but after her experience with the police officer she hadn't gone back to her parent's house. Maria could often tell when Jaz was missing her parents and always encouraged her to keep hoping that things would work out.

"I spent four years looking out my living room window hoping Lisa would come home. And now, it was worth every day because of how it worked out. Don't lose hope Jazzy girl!"

In the middle of December Maria's rheumatoid arthritis flared, and Jaz realized just how much Maria's help meant to her business. Suddenly faced with handling bookings, the contractors doing her sewing, and all the online inquiries about clothes, along with feeling sick to her stomach to have Maria in so much pain, Jaz struggled to cope.

The first day, Carla wasn't able to get away from work early, so Jaz added watching Becky to her schedule. The bus dropped her off about half a block away, and Jaz just made it in time to see Becky let off. Becky used the sign for 'Maria' and Jaz had to tell her that Maria was sick.

When they got to the house Becky wanted to climb in bed with her friend, but Jaz could tell Maria was in too much pain for that. She spent the afternoon bribing Becky with cookies to try to keep her distracted and out of Maria's room.

When Carla walked in the door, Jaz nearly cried with relief. "Thank goodness you're home! Becky really wants to be with Maria, but she's in so much pain I didn't think it was a good idea. Um, and I gave Becky a lot of cookies..."

Becky left her mom's side to come over and stroke Jaz's hair — her way of showing Jaz how much she liked her. "Yeah yeah, but would you like me as much without the cookies?" Jaz teased.

With a shake of her head 'no' Becky went back over to the cupboard where the cookies were. "Enough of that missy," her mom said firmly, "Let's go downstairs now." She turned to Jaz, "You were an absolute life saver today. Thank you so much. Tomorrow Chris will be back before Becky gets home... As soon as he's home tonight I'll come check on Maria. And Lisa should be home soon."

Jaz nodded, and went straight to Maria's room when they left. She felt so helpless watching Maria suffer, but didn't want to leave her alone.

"I'll be OK," Maria whispered, "You go take care of your business. I spent lots of days alone in bed before you came." She tried to smile, but it came across as more of a grimace.

With tears in her eyes, Jaz quietly left the room, but she struggled to focus. Maria was such a comforting, stable person to be around. Without her, Jaz felt lost. When Lisa finally arrived home she had caught up with all the messages and booking that Maria normally handled, and then set the table while Lisa heated up some frozen dinners.

"I've learned to do as little as possible when Mom's like this, so I hope you're OK with frozen dinners for a few days."

"Yeah, of course. I just... it's so hard to not be able to do anything for her. How do you handle it?"

Lisa brought the steaming containers over to the table, and sat down with a sigh, "It feels impossible every time. It's so unfair that just when Mom gets her life back, and we have so much to look forward to that her body does this to her. She deserves way better."

"Ooof!" Jaz gently rubbed her belly.

"You OK?"

"Yeah, sorry. This guy's really getting the kicks in lately." Jaz couldn't help but smile. Even though the kicks were almost getting painful, she loved knowing her baby was strong. But then her face fell. "What do I if your mom can't go with me to prenatal classes? We're supposed to start right after Christmas. I'm sorry. That's super selfish."

"Not at all. It's important! If Mom's not well, I'll take time off to stay with her, and Lauren or Carla can go with you."

"Seriously? You'd do that for me?" The old feelings of being a burden and a failure started to creep back in. Jaz felt terrible that her life would impact other people's lives. "I can go alone...but I don't want to leave Maria."

"Jaz, stop it. We're all in this together and it's going to be OK. Mom has been so much happier since she started working for you. That's worth everything to me—and her! So just let us help where we can, OK?"

The baby kicked again and Jaz laughed. "I think he just told me to get over myself and let you help!"

Lisa reached over and rubbed the rippling belly, "I like him more every day!" she looked at Jaz thoughtfully. "What will you do if it's a girl?"

"I guess it'll be OK. I just think it will be harder to raise a girl differently than I was raised. Which is what I really want—you know, to be chill about stuff and not to pressure her too much. But with a boy I feel like it will be different."

"You know I can't help with all the parenting stuff. But I bet I'll be really good at spoiling him. Or her."

Jaz smiled, "I'm so lucky to have you guys."

CHAPTER 24

*O*n December 23rd, the lady who asked to be paid in cash brought Jaz a beautiful handmade baby quilt. It left Jaz speechless. Never in her life had she received such a personal gift. She stood in the entryway holding the quilt in one hand after taking it out of the Christmas gift bag.

"Wow... Susan... this is just... it's gorgeous." Jaz ran her hand across the softest fabric she had every touched. The images on the fabric were all vintage farm scenes.

"It's something I started to make for my own grandchildren years ago, but my daughter didn't want anything homemade. I thought you might like it, and it's been so much fun to work on. It's not much compared to all you've done for me, but I wanted to do something to say thank you. I'm going to spend this last Christmas helping my daughter out, and then I'll be looking for my own place. The income from sewing for you... it's changing my life."

"I think it's time for a cup of tea," Maria interrupted. "Come on, let's all go sit down."

They followed her to the table where Lisa was working on her freelance bookkeeping. She moved her things to the side and got up to help her mom. "I'm ready for a break, anyways."

Once they all had their tea, and Maria placed a plate of Christmas cookies from the bakery on the table she turned to Susan. "We'd love to hear your story."

Susan looked down for a minute before lifting her gaze and smiling at the ladies around the table. "My husband left me four years ago. I didn't have a job or anything, and ended up with nowhere to go so my daughter said I could live with her and her family. It... she's not... I didn't do such a good job raising her I guess. Between helping with the kids, and doing the housework and cooking now, it just feels like I'm a slave. And whenever I tried to tell her or her husband that it was too much, they'd remind me what a burden it was to have to take care of me."

"What? That's terrible!" Maria could immediately understand the manipulation she was experiencing.

"I've been trying to find a way to get my own place for a while." she turned to Maria, "When we met at that computer class at the library, that was my first time doing something on my own. And having all of you to visit with every week was a lifeline for me."

She turned to Jaz, "And then when you offered to pay me to do the one thing I've always loved to do, it was like a miracle from heaven! I've been saving almost everything. I have enough money to, um, reimburse my daughter for the cost of my food for the past few months. I'll give that to them as soon as I have a place to move to."

"It sounds like you've been more than paying your way with everything you do for them," Lisa observed.

"Thank you. I've tried to be helpful. And I thought once the kids were all in school I'd have it a little easier. But they just keep expecting more of me. I do love them, it's just time for me to find my own way."

"Wow," Jaz breathed, "You're really brave to be doing all of this. If you'd like, I can have more work for you."

"I can't fit any more in right now. But as soon as I'm on my own, I'd love more. It's so much fun to get paid to sew! And you come up with the most interesting ideas!"

"Well, you do really good work. If my grandma was around, she'd give you her approval for sure."

"That's quite the compliment. Maria's told me all about what she taught you."

"I wish I didn't have so many bookings for the other bedroom, then you could just stay here!" For the very first time, Lisa was regretting her Airbnb plan. If that bedroom was empty, she'd be in a position to help someone else out. Of course, all of the guests appreciated their place, and the comfortable feeling that seemed to come with staying there, but it wasn't quite the same as helping someone who really needed to get out of a bad situation. She suspected Susan's home life was much worse than she was letting on.

"Oh, I'll be alright." Susan put a brave smile on her face, and changed the topic. "Now, Jaz, tell me all about your plans for your little one."

Jaz recognized the topic change, but was happy to go along. She knew Maria would continue to look out for her friend, and would let Jaz know if there was anything else they could do for her.

As they ate supper later that day, Jaz kept thinking about Susan's situation. "Is that how you felt Maria, when you were with your husband? Like you needed to leave but had nowhere to go and no way to pay for yourself?"

"Very much so. And when you don't have any employable skills, or any way to support yourself, it's worse. Having to rely on someone for everything—especially when that person doesn't like you—it's so degrading."

"Are there lots of women like that?"

"Well, I imagine men *and* women. Although mostly women. You know, I get a feeling when I'm chatting with other people sometimes. There's another lady from our library group that may be in a similar situation. And perhaps a gentleman too. I mean, I don't think he has to cook and clean like Susan does, but I don't think he's very happy living with his kids. It's so sad."

"What can we do about it?"

"Do? What do you mean?"

"It's a problem, right? People living places where they're trapped and they're not treated right? Shouldn't we try to help them?" Jaz thought back to the one day she spent wandering around the city until Kara rescued her. Now, even though she still desperately missed her parents, she was in a beautiful, safe place, surrounded by people who genuinely cared about her. "I mean, we're good, right? We're all making money and doing what we want. So maybe we could help someone else be OK...Somehow..."

"Oh Jaz, I'm so proud of you! You're just like Lisa, you know? Always trying to make life better for others."

"I don't know about that. I've never even thought about what life must be like for others until now. It's just that I feel like I *have* to do something about it."

A huge smile lit up Lisa's face, "I don't know what's going on here, but I feel like we're onto something. I wish Carrie was done school. She'd understand more about how to reach out to people that need help. But I'm pretty sure we could start planning for *something*. And then when she graduates at the end of April we'll grab her!"

It wasn't much of a plan yet, but all three of them felt like they were on the edge of something important. With a feeling of anticipation, Maria feeling much better, and Christmas just around the corner, they were all ready for whatever they could come up with next.

Christmas morning Jaz lay in bed and relaxed instead of forcing herself to get up and start working right away. Maria had insisted they shut everything down from the 24th until the new year, and after a bit of resistance Jaz had agreed. All her regular clients had bought their Christmas outfits weeks ago, and after a short 'business meeting', Jaz, Maria, and Lisa had decided there was no need for Jaz to run any sales after Christmas either. She had more than enough business at her regular prices to not need to give any discounts.

Struggling to get up thanks to her bulging belly, Jaz walked over and looked at her phone. Nothing. She had done two things yesterday. First, she had battled the mall crowds to go into the phone store and take over payments for her cell phone and set it up to be paid from her business account. Then she ordered a huge Christmas flower arrangement to be delivered to her parents, and another one for Maria and Lisa.

The flower shop hadn't called to say they couldn't make the delivery, so she knew her parents had received her gift. But they hadn't texted or called. She fought off a wave of disappointment. It didn't matter. Maria kept telling her not to lose hope and she wouldn't. Even if it took ten years of sending flowers to her mom, she was determined that one day they'd want to see her again. She got dressed and went downstairs to celebrate Christmas with her closest friends.

On Boxing Day Lisa and Maria insisted Jaz join them for their friend's annual Boxing Day party. "They do it every year," Lisa explained, "On my first Christmas here alone they insisted I join them, and it was so much fun. I've gone ever since."

"How do you know them?"

"Well, Manuel was working as a janitor at an office building, and when he retired, I got the job and he trained me. Him and his wife Betsy kind of took me under their wing, and when Mom moved here too they helped out. You'll love them. Their oldest son Freddy is taking business classes and does the janitor stuff now, and Marco is in his last year of high school. The boys' parents were murdered in Central America, and Manuel and Betsy adopted the boys when they were little and brought them back here. The whole family are a blast to hang out with."

Lisa wasn't exaggerating, as Jaz found herself surrounded by Betsy and her sisters as soon as she walked in the door. She was given a stool to sit on at the kitchen island while the ladies all finished the food preparations, and constantly offered tastes of everything they were making. "I won't have room to eat later!" she protested as she laughingly tried to slow the tide of food.

"Good luck with that!" Lisa walked into the kitchen with a glass of wine, "The first year I was here my plate almost broke in half with all the food they put on it!"

"You really haven't eaten a real meal until you've had our food," bragged Betsy, "So we have a lot to make up for the first time you come in the door."

That night Jaz fell into bed still full from dinner and with a happy heart. She couldn't help but feel good being around Manuel and Betsy and their family. And even though Jaz saw herself as an outsider, they had made her feel very welcome. A few of the aunties even insisted Jaz take their numbers in case she needed a babysitter later on. And, after admiring the stylish outfits Lisa and Maria were wearing courtesy of Jaz, those that had Instagram immediately started to follow her and like her posts.

Jaz said a silent thank you to Maria for insisting they all take a break from the business. It was always a thrill to create things and sell them to happy clients, but Jaz put a lot of pressure on herself to constantly improve the business and increase her sales. A week off gave her time to rest, and spend time researching ideas. She fell asleep with ideas for new clothing lines filling her dreams.

CHAPTER 25

Two of Jaz's contractors chose to continue working over the holidays, so by the time she opened up her page to purchases again she had a good supply of clothing ready to sell. Although her jean jackets were still popular, she slowed down to only doing one per week, and charging $145. The decrease in supply made each jacket get snatched up right away no matter what size it was. Sometimes she was shocked by what people were willing to pay, but then she remembered how her mom felt about always having the 'right' clothes.

More and more of her followers were asking for items to be shipped, so she worked together with Lisa and Maria to set up a system. Jaz didn't want to be in charge of shipping, and Maria found that wrapping up packages was too hard on her hands. Carla in the middle of cleaning the upstairs when they were talking about it, and she offered to do it.

"I'd love a chance to earn a bit of extra money, and I can drop things off at the post office on my way to work every day." It was an ideal situation that everyone was happy with. Chris and Carla were working hard and saving every penny they could in the hopes that soon they'd be able to buy a fixer upper and use it as a showpiece for their construction business. "Chris has been working with a partner on flipping a house. If it goes well, we could even be back to running our own business next year! And it'll be nice for me to have some extra income too!"

Carla was soon spending hours every week working for the Jazzy Clothing Company. Everyone joked that the basement was actually the shipping and receiving department, and the main floor had become the accounting and marketing department. There was definitely a sense of busyness and purpose, but Jaz was becoming concerned that her business was taking over Lisa and Maria's house.

She really needed more space to set up the week's work for each of her contractors, and her own work tended to spill into the upstairs hallway when she was on a roll. Often she had to hurriedly tidy up before Airbnb guests checked in so they wouldn't be put off by piles of clothes everywhere.

But before she could think of a solution her days became entirely full with preparing for the baby coming. Maria happily signed up to be her birthing coach, and was able to join Jaz for all but one of the prenatal classes. She came down with the flu, and Lauren stepped in to cover for her.

"Geez, you are going to be *set* for labor!" she said later at the coffee shop Jaz insisted on taking her to. "I didn't do any of this stuff before having Brittany and I was seriously freaked out. Kara was good with helping me feel a bit better when I finally got in to see her, but labor is some seriously crazy shit when you don't know what's going on."

"Wait, Kara the physician's assistant?"

"The one and only."

"Wow, she gets around! She's the one who took me to Carrie's the day my parents kicked me out."

"And Carrie introduced me to Kara after we moved in to Carrie's old place. Small world, huh?"

"So you don't think labor will be that bad for me?"

Lauren gave her a sideways glance before snorting out a laugh, "Oh, it's gonna be the worst thing ever. And then it's the best thing ever. I was pissed off about being pregnant, but having Brittany rocks. Especially after the first couple months. Wouldn't change it for anything."

Jaz smiled, and then grunted as her baby resumed his evening kicking routine. "I swear, the less energy I have the more energy he has. I tried to nap today because I just couldn't do anymore work. But as soon as I lay down he started beating on me!"

"You're so small. He probably needs more room. How much longer?"

"Three more weeks. I hope he's not late. Or early. I still have to get all his baby stuff. We were going to go out shopping last weekend, but there was so much to do for the business that we were kept busy the whole time. And then in the evenings Maria and I were both too tired to go out."

"What do you need?"

"Everything! Well, I have enough clothes," she giggled, "I have way more than enough baby clothes. But aside from a baby blanket I got as a gift, I don't have anything."

"Sweet! I'll hook you up. After I had Brittany, all of Carrie's friends gave us stuff and she's outgrown all of it. Except, if you can afford it, you should get a new car seat. I heard you're not supposed to use those for too long."

"Seriously? That would be fantastic! Thank you so much!"

"No problem! Hey, how about you make sure nobody comes on Saturday afternoon and I'll bring it all over and show you how to use it."

"OK…" Jaz pulled out her phone, "I messaged Maria. She sets up all the appointments, so she'll know if we have anything booked."

"How does that work with her? Is it a pain to have her around all the time?"

"Are you kidding? She's fantastic! Her official title is Executive Assistant, but really she helps me with everything. In fact, I just gave her another raise because she's so amazing. Between her and Lisa they take care of all the business stuff, and I get to spend my time creating. It's perfect."

"Kinda like how Carrie sells all my paintings so I don't have to bother with it."

"Yeah, like that!"

CHAPTER 26

Saturday afternoon Maria asked Jaz to drive over to the bakery and pick up a few things before Lauren came. Jaz was happy to get out of the house. They had been busy all morning so that they could take the afternoon off, and she was feeling overwhelmed.

When she walked into the house she was shocked to see almost everyone she knew in the living room. "Surprise!" Lauren shouted, "Welcome to your baby shower!"

"My what?"

"Your baby shower silly! We are going to make a stink about you and give you tons of sh—stuff for your baby!"

"Seriously?" Slowly Jaz walked into the room. Carrie and Katie were there, along with Kara, Betsy and her sisters, Carla, Lauren, Lisa, and Maria. "You guys are the best."

They placed her on the couch and all gathered around her for some visiting before Lisa called them to grab snacks. Somehow they had come up with a table full of appetizers, and even a baby themed cake! Jaz took pictures of everything before sitting down with her own plate of food.

The pile of presents was overwhelming—she'd never had more than a friend or two over for birthday parties, and Christmas was quiet as an only child. Now, she was the center of some very enthusiastic attention. Katie came to Princess Jasmine's rescue, and brought her gifts one at a time to open.

Every gift was special, but she was especially pleased with Carrie and Kara's gift. It was a fully stocked hospital bag with everything she might need while at the hospital. She had seen a few things on Pinterest about hospital bags, but hadn't read them yet. Now she didn't have to worry about not being prepared!

After everyone left, Lauren helped her set up a bassinet and change table in her bedroom, and showed her where to put things so she'd have easy access to it all. It made the room feel crowded, but Lauren assured her having everything close by was a good thing.

"For the first week you're gonna feel like you need more arms. But then it starts to get better."

"Lauren?"

"Yeah babe?"

"Um, thanks for everything. For all the stuff, and having a baby shower, and answering my questions. I really appreciate it!"

"No prob! And no matter what, I'm just a text away. Got it?"

"Got it!"

That night, Lauren got to put her promise into action.

> 11:23 pm: *Lauren? I think I'm in labor! It feels like someone's grabbing my belly with bear claws and pinching!*

> 11:25 pm: *lol! yeah, that sounds like labor. how far apart are they?*

11:26 pm: *I went to bed at 11 and I've had two since.*

11:27 pm: *anything before that?*

11:35 pm: *Just had another one. My back's been hurting like crazy today, but no labor pains*

11:36 pm: *babe I think those were labor pains too. get lisa. love ya*

11:37 pm: *thx love you too*

At her house, Lauren smiled before texting Carrie and Kara. If Jaz wasn't using proper punctuation or grammar anymore, she was definitely in labor.

12:57 am: *what room u in*

1:14 am: *Sorry, took a while to check in. I'm in 1429. Lisa and Maria are here. I can't...*

Again Lauren smiled. She had just arrived at the hospital with Carrie and Kara. They had to wait for Jonathan to come over to watch Carrie's kids before they could leave, but all three had agreed at Christmas that they wouldn't let Jaz go through labor alone.

"Carrie! You didn't bring your laptop with you! What's wrong?"

"Very funny!" Carrie yawned, "Tonight, or this morning, or whatever this is, is all about Jaz. No studying allowed."

Together they made their way up to the maternity ward. It was a quiet night, and the nurses allowed them all to crowd into Jaz's room. She was obviously in the middle of a contraction and instead of her usual smile they were treated to a silent grimace. Maria and Lisa were on each side of her holding her hands, and Maria was talking quietly to her. When the contraction passed, everyone in the room let out a breath.

"Hey!" Jaz managed a weak smile, "Fancy seeing you here!"

"Wouldn't miss it for the world. I told you that kid needed more space! Looks like he's gonna start life in a hurry."

"Dear Lord, I sure hope so!" Maria reached up and brushed Jaz's bangs aside. "This girl's a silent sufferer, but she'd definitely in a lot of pain."

They all made themselves as comfortable as they could, and for the next five hours they suffered along with Jaz as her contractions continued without her labor progressing. The nurses seemed unconcerned but eventually even Kara was getting antsy for something to happen.

6:41 am Jaz: *I'm scared*

6:41 am Lauren: *we've got ur back babe. hang in there. ur doin awesome*

Lauren looked up at Jaz. From the outside Jaz looked exhausted, but not scared. She guessed that Jaz was trying to be brave and that's why she texted instead of telling everyone what she was feeling. Although she had no idea why. She tried to figure out a way to tell Jaz it was OK.

"You know, when I was in labor I made so much noise one of the nurses told me off! She said to save some of my energy for delivery. So, Jaz, care to let a few f-bombs rip? You know, let off some steam?"

Jaz gave a weak smile and shook her head 'no'. Kara slipped out of the room and came back a few minutes later with a nurse.

"So Miss Lee, you've got quite the support group here! How about they all step out for a minute so I can check you out?"

Jaz's eyes widened and she shook her head no, "Please, can Maria stay?"

"Oh, it this your mom?"

"Pretty much, yeah."

The nurse paused for a moment, "Alright. The rest of you ladies, why don't you grab a coffee and a bite to eat and come back in a bit. It looks like you could all use a little pick-me-up."

They all hugged Jaz before reluctantly leaving. As soon as they had coffees and muffins they all went back up to the maternity ward.

"Is something wrong?" Lauren finally asked Kara.

"I don't know. I'm worried that she's getting so weak. It's not unusual for labour to drag out like this, but it seems like she's fading and I don't like it."

"That's what I thought too," Carrie admitted, "But I didn't want to worry her by saying anything."

"She's pretty freaked out right now, she texted me that she's scared. I think she didn't want to say it out loud."

The door to Jaz's room was still closed when they got there, but Kara confidently knocked and then slowly opened the door. The nurse was just removing her gloves. "Good news ladies! She's almost fully dilated now." She turned to Jaz, "You've got some work to do soon, but you're on your way. I'm going to send the doctor in to see you as soon as she's free."

"Will that be long?" Maria asked.

"No, she's just grabbing a bite to eat herself. You're the first ones she'll visit."

They all breathed a sigh of relief, and then held their breath again while Jaz suffered silently through another contraction.

"Was that one way longer?" Lauren asked, "Because I was ready to pass out!"

"They're definitely getting longer. The nurse noticed too when she was in here. Jazzy girl, it won't be much longer now!" Maria continued to stroke Jaz's hair, and her eyes quickly closed. "She's so tired," Maria whispered.

The doctor arrived just as another contraction woke Jaz up. "No bearing down ladies!" she joked, "Hemorrhoids are a serious problem for those who insist on straining when their friends are in labor!"

Her cheerful approach helped lighten the atmosphere in the room, and she looked at Jaz's chart before smiling. "I'll bet it's felt like forever, but things should start to move now—literally! I'd like to move you into the birthing room soon, but I'll let you all have a few more minutes together before we do that."

Tears glistened in Jaz's eyes, "Can't I stay here? Please?"

The doctor gently took Jaz's hands, "We're going to take good care of you, but part of that means we need to have a slightly better set up than what's offered in your room." She looked down at the chart again, "Which one of you is Maria?"

"Oh, that's me!"

"OK, Maria will stay with you the whole time, and I'm pretty sure your friends will be right at the door as close to you as possible." They all agreed.

When Jaz was wheeled away there wasn't a dry eye among the group. They all stood as close to Jaz as they could get—just like the doctor predicted.

Finally, after what felt like a frightening amount of time they heard a primal scream come from the room followed a few seconds later by the miraculous sound of a newborn baby's first cry. They all slumped against the wall in relief.

A few minutes later a nurse opened the door and walked out with Maria. "It's a boy!" she stated beaming before nearly collapsing against the nurse. Lisa was at her side immediately and almost carried her to the nearest chair. "I'm OK," Maria promised, "Just completely spent."

The nurse stood looking at Maria for a moment before turning to the ladies. "You're all able to come in for a very short visit in ten or fifteen minutes. Then I think perhaps everyone needs to go home and get some rest."

"Is Jaz OK?" This from Lauren.

"Yes, she's OK, but it was a very difficult delivery. We'll keep her here for at least a full day, maybe two, until she's strong enough to get around safely."

When they were allowed into the birthing suite they were greeted by the site of a very pale Jaz with a bassinet right beside her. She smiled weakly, "You're right," she whispered, "It's worth it. Meet Alexander Stanley Lee."

Lisa looked at her in surprise, "Your dad's name is Stanley!"

Jaz nodded and smiled, "One day he'll meet his grandpa."

By the time they all had a chance to admire Alexander, Jaz was asleep, and they quietly walked out. The nurse brought over a wheelchair for Maria. "I know you say you're fine, but that was quite the marathon you ran today. Save your energy and get a ride to the car."

Lisa gave her a grateful look before helping her mom into the chair. "Come on grandma, let's get you home and rested up before that little guy interrupts our nights with his hollering."

CHAPTER 27

"*H*ey little guy! It's time for our walk!" Five week old Alexander was already completely captivated by his mom's face and voice. He smiled and flapped his hands.

Jaz sighed with happiness as she picked up her son and snuggled him into that perfectly sized spot between her neck and her shoulder. Now that she had healed from giving birth she was enjoying almost every moment with him. Although he woke up at least once every night, he settled quickly as he nursed, and then often slept until seven.

The new schedule was slowly sorting itself out. After getting him up and fed Jaz would bring him downstairs to see Lisa and Maria while she got herself some tea and breakfast. It took Maria almost as long to recover from Alex's delivery as Jaz, but Jaz brought him into her room every afternoon to sleep beside her on the bed. She claimed his little baby snores were like therapy, and now they were all feeling much more like themselves. On the few instances they had all gone out, Maria continued to use a wheelchair but she was always happy to have Alex in her lap, making it possible to Jaz for take them both on out on her own.

After breakfast Jaz would spend as much time as possible sewing, or getting the next projects ready for her contractors before Alex needed her attention again. Then she would bundle him up and take him for a walk in the stroller Lauren lent her. Every day her route was the same, passing her parent's house twice before finally making her way back home. Sometimes on the weekends she thought she saw the curtains twitch, but she was never quite sure.

In the afternoons, Maria would watch Alex while Jaz had client visits, and then when it was time for Becky to get home from school, Jaz would spend her time with Alex—often on the main level with Becky and Maria. Becky was in awe of her new little friend, and would spend up to an hour just sitting beside him and stroking his cheek and hair.

As Lauren predicted, Jaz quickly got the hang of caring for a newborn on top of running her business. She knew she couldn't do it without Maria and Lisa's help, but they assured her that she was more than capable.

Then, when Alex went to bed for the night Jaz would sew until she couldn't keep her eyes open anymore. She was making more than enough to easily support herself and Alex—even if they were living on their own—but she wanted to build the business as big as possible to be ready for whatever the ladies decided to do to help others. Susan was still living with her daughter and son-in-law. They insisted she stay for a few more months until they could find after-school care for the kids. She claimed it was fine, but every week she looked tired.

Jaz hired three more ladies to help with the sewing, but decided that one of them couldn't produce the quality needed. Maria offered to be the one to talk to her, but Jaz refused. She spent hours reading online about how to fire people before deciding on the nicest, but firmest way to let her go. In the end, the lady seemed relieved, and Jaz could add another business 'chore' to the growing list of things she could now do.

Second only to Alex's arrival was Lisa's big news. Effective April 30th she would no longer be working at the commercial real estate company. While Maria and Jaz had known for a while that Lisa wasn't enjoying her work, the announcement still came as a happy surprise.

"I know it's a bit unusual to give a full month's notice, but I want to leave them in the best position possible. There's a new bookkeeper who joined the team last month who's quite experienced. I think he'll be able to take over a lot of my duties with some training."

"Well, maybe that solves one of my problems, too." Jaz admitted, "I've been getting way behind on my part of the bookkeeping for the business. All I know for sure is how much we pay the contractors every week. Can I hire you as the company's CFO?"

"What's that?" Maria wondered.

"Chief Financial Officer—I read all about it online. Lisa could take over all the financial stuff. Maybe even paying the contractors? It's a lot more work than it used to be." She giggled, "But you'll have to figure out what to pay yourself. Hey, that should be your first task!"

"Are you sure? Sometimes it's easier to have someone who's a little removed from the business to handle the finances." Lisa wanted nothing more than to be a part of the excitement of the Jazzy Clothing Company. But she had already prepared herself to take on more freelance clients and keep her distance if Jaz wanted to bring in someone else to do it.

"I've been thinking about it for a while. I just didn't want to ask too much of you. But as soon as you're done with the firm, you're definitely the only person I want handling our finances."

"You're really becoming a lot more confident, you know that?"

"Yeah, apparently surviving being banished from your childhood home, starting a business, and then having a baby makes you stronger!" Her smile was bittersweet. "I already ordered a bouquet to send my mom for Mother's Day. Maybe this time…"

Just then Maria's phone rang. "Hello? Oh, Jonathan!"

Lisa and Jaz exchanged glances. Why would Carrie's boyfriend be calling Maria?

After she hung up, she turned to them with a huge smile, "Jonathan's up to something! He's planning a party for Carrie at the end of the month when she finishes school. And he wants me to find the best hotel in the city for wheelchairs so he can surprise her by booking Carrie's parents in there for that whole weekend!"

"He's super considerate. And I know Carrie has been wishing her mom could visit her here. It's hard with a wheelchair I guess. By why a surprise? Is it just because she's so busy right now? When I went over last week with Alex she was actually studying at the library and Jonathan was watching the kids so I didn't even get to see how she's doing."

Lisa saw her chance to hang out with Alex—the only baby she'd ever met that she actually liked. "Well, whatever he's planning, he wants Carrie's parents there. I think this is a great time for you two to get out on your own and let me have Alex to myself. If you go on Saturday I'll babysit. There's no way you can check out hotels with a baby and a wheelchair."

Jaz surprised herself by agreeing right away, "I guess this will be my first time going out anywhere without him! It's weird. But I'm already looking forward to it! I'll make a list of the hotels that say they're accessible and we'll go test drive them all. Ooohhh, we should go out for coffee too!"

"OK, it's definitely time you got out more when you get excited about a cup coffee!" Lisa laughed and then became thoughtful, "You know, you spend all your time with people who are way older than you. Do you ever miss hanging out with people your own age?"

"I miss feeling carefree I guess. You know, hanging out without any responsibilities. But I don't think anyone my age would get me. Everything's different. They'd be talking about crushes and grades while I'm breastfeeding Alex and planning a clothing line. It just wouldn't work."

CHAPTER 28

"*I* think this is the one!" Maria wheeled herself into and out of the shower, and then out of the bathroom and over to the bed. "It's exhausting to wheel myself, but at least in this room it's easy to get everywhere.

Jaz agreed, "I had no idea it was so hard to find an accessible hotel room! That first place would've been OK if there was actually a ramp from the handicap parking to the sidewalk, but some of the others. Geez."

"You know, it's different for me because I *can* stand up and move myself, even when I'm having a bad day. But for someone who can't do that… I don't know which of the other rooms was worse, the one with a bed you needed to climb up on, or the one with the bathroom you couldn't turn a wheelchair around in. This is by far the best one."

"OK, so let's go back to reception and call Jonathan. I read in one of the accessibility blogs that sometimes the hotel gives away the accessible room after you've booked it so I want to make sure they book it with us right there. Although I'm guessing if their room is this well-designed then they aren't likely to mess up the booking."

Half an hour later Jaz and Maria were enjoying lunch at the hotel's restaurant after successfully helping book the room for Carrie's parents.

"I feel weird without Alex. Like my arms are all floppy or something."

"You're doing such a good job with him!" Maria never missed a chance to compliment her girls on everything they were doing right.

Without Alex to distract them, the conversation turned to the business, and Susan. "She's really our best worker. I wish we had a place we could set her up in. You know, where she had a sewing room with good lighting, and a separate area where she could just relax and not have to slave for her family."

"That's a good idea! We could buy a whole apartment building and set it up for people like Susan, and that guy you met at the library who hides out there away from his family all day."

"Wouldn't that be fun? Then we'd hire Chris to renovate all the apartments, and make a couple of them accessible..."

"Do you think people in wheelchairs have a harder time renting a place? I never thought about that before. But after this morning, there's so many little things about a building that can make it harder to get around."

"I remember when Lisa was looking for a place to buy, a lot of the houses she looked at were impossible to adapt—even with money to do it. And having my bathroom fully accessible finally gave me back some dignity because I can do almost everything myself now."

"Was the bathroom like that when she bought it?"

"Heavens no! It was a disaster—the whole house was. But Lisa, in typical style, attacked the renovations head on and had the house ready for us in less than two months. Actually, my bathroom was the biggest hold up in the end, because everything had to be ordered in."

"Hmmm..." A dreamy smile spread across Jaz's face, "I wonder if it's actually possible to buy an apartment building. Do you know how much they cost?"

"No, but I think your CFO will be able to figure that all out for you. I'm so excited that soon we'll all be working together every day. *You* Jazzy girl are changing our lives!"

They paused their conversation when the waitress came. Jaz happily dug into her burger, and Maria started on her bowl of clam chowder.

"Ah," Jaz sat back in her chair, "I am so full. And I need to get back to nurse Alex." She hunched her shoulders. "Not everything about motherhood is smiles and cuddles."

Maria smiled sympathetically. Being around Jaz brought back some of her own memories about having Lisa. Not all the memories were good—her husband had been selfish and mean from day one—but there were some good memories with Lisa that had been buried for years. She hoped that Jaz would never get trapped in a relationship that made her life worse.

Just as they were getting ready to leave Jaz's phone pinged. "Hey, Lauren's coming over with Brittany in a bit. I guess we should get going."

Lauren continued to visit Jaz and help her out with Alex's changing needs. She didn't always bring Brittany. Now in full toddler stage, Brittany tended to tear around the house chattering a mile a minute when she wasn't trying to pick up Alex. The first time she met her newest little friend, Lauren told her his name was Alexander. That was too much of a mouthful for her, and she shortened his name to Ander which she loved to holler the second she was in the door.

Today was no exception. "Ander! My Ander!" she shouted, and Lauren barely had time to get Brittany's shoes off before she ran into the living room looking for him. Jaz was just finishing nursing him, and he was content to watch her try to jump up and down in front of him while Jaz burped him.

As soon as she was done Lauren took him, and Brittany climbed into

Jaz's lap. "I can't believe Alex will ever be this big!" she admitted. She hadn't been around any little children growing up, and everything Alex or Brittany did continued to amaze her. Seconds later Brittany was off her lap and over to Maria.

"I can't pick you up today lovey, but shall we get you a cookie?" Together the two of them went to the kitchen.

Lisa sighed, "You guys are the best! Mom's so happy having babies around she's finally quit bugging me about having my own!"

"Still on the single lady bandwagon, huh?"

"Definitely!"

"I'm gonna laugh so hard when you fall for some dude."

Jaz smiled too, "I can't even imagine a guy for you... but yeah. If you ever do fall in love, we're never going to let you live it down."

Maria came back in the room with Brittany eating cookies from both hands, and Jaz changed the topic. "Does anyone know what Jonathan's planning for Carrie's party? Seems like it must be something big if he's bringing her parents down to surprise her."

"I doubt she'll even be able to stay awake for it. When I was there the other day to drop off paintings she looked like crap. I hope this is all worth it."

"It will be," Maria stated confidently, "She didn't need grad school to be able to help people—she does that naturally—but strangers aren't going to pay to work with her without the degree to back her up."

They agreed with her, but felt for Carrie as she pushed through her last few weeks of grad school. At least Jonathan was nearby to help her out with the kids.

"I'm going to make a dress for her to wear to the party! If she's that busy she won't have time for shopping, and she needs something new to wear to celebrate her new start."

"Cool! What about Matthew and Katie too?"

"Yeah! For sure!"

That night Jaz found the perfect dress for Carrie in her supply of clothes waiting for alterations. It was a white, floor-length cotton dress with eyelet lace around the neck and hem, and white straps over the shoulders. She hung it up on the corner of the mirror in the sewing room and stepped back to take a look.

It definitely needed to be shortened to above the knee. Jaz could already picture darts at the waist to highlight Carrie's figure, and taking it in around the bodice to fit better. She'd reuse the lace on the shorter hem. But it still needed something… her eye caught a bright blue length of fabric left over from a men's-dress-shirt-turned-women's-dress project. Perfect! A fabric belt in that bright color. And Jaz would suggest Carrie wear the same jewelry and shoes they bought for her green dress last year.

CHAPTER 29

The day of the party Jaz left Alex with Maria and drove to Carrie's with the new outfits.

"Jaz! Come on in!" Carrie was holding a cup of coffee, and her hair was still damp from a shower. She was wearing a pair of khaki shorts and a t-shirt of Jaz's design that said 'rockin Mom' in cut out letters.

"Cute shirt!"

"Thanks to you! Katie! Matthew! Jaz is here!"

Both kids ran up from downstairs.

"No Alex?" Katie pouted.

"Not this time. But I brought new clothes for the party tonight!"

"YAY!" Katie yelled.

"Honestly Jaz. How do you always know when I need rescuing? I planned on shopping today, and then changed my mind because I don't want to go out. The kids are growing so fast right now."

Jaz came in and laid the clothes over the couch before turning and hugging everyone. "I've got something for all of you!"

"Oh, I was going to wear the green dress you made me last year!"

"Not a chance! Here, this is for you…" She held out the dress and Carrie went to the kitchen and put down her mug before coming back and taking it from Jaz.

"Oh my gosh. I *love* it! And the bright blue belt—too fun! I'll go try it on right now!"

"Remember the necklace Mommy!" Katie called after her. "Whatcha got for me Princess Jasmine?"

"For you I have grey sweatpants and a black t-shirt!"

Katie's mouth dropped open in horror before she realized Jaz was teasing. "No you don't!"

Jaz pretended to sigh, "You're just too smart for me! Ok, Ok, here's yours!" She held out an asymmetrical pink top with little white bows down the angled hem, and a silver tutu-type skirt to go underneath it. For any other girl, it was more a dress-up costume than an outfit. For Katie, it was perfect. She ran off to try it on.

Matthew's outfit was far more understated. Jaz found a pair of navy boater shorts with a subtle sailboat design across them that she bought online. It was paired with a white button-up shirt that she added yellow accents to, and a blue and white striped bow tie. She also found a pair of brown leather loafers on eBay that she hoped would be the right size. "Do the shoes fit?"

"Yeah, they're perfect Jaz! Oh, but what socks do I wear with them?"

"If it doesn't bother you, I'd go with no socks. That's kinda a thing for guys wearing loafers right now."

"Cool!" He followed Carrie and Katie upstairs to try it all on, and Carrie passed him coming down the stairs.

The dress fit her perfectly, and there was a little twinkle in her eye that hadn't been there when she opened the door. "Jaz, I don't know how you do it. It feels so nice just to have something new to wear. And it's prettier than *anything* I could have found in the store. Thank you!"

"You know, that orange chunky necklace totally works! Is that what Katie was talking about?"

"Yeah, she grabbed it at a thrift store a while ago and then gave it to me for Mother's Day. I have to admit, I've worn it a lot more than I expected!" She turned to watch Katie dance down the stairs in her new outfit, followed by Matthew. "Holy cow! Does Jaz know you guys or what? I shouldn't be surprised anymore, but you definitely manage to go over the top when you dress us. And those shoes Matthew! Jonathan's going to be jealous!"

Matthew looked down at his feet and grinned, "I love this outfit! I can't wait to show Jonathan!"

"Well, we'll see him soon enough." She looked at Jaz, "I've been told not to show up until six tonight. I don't know what he's planning, but I'm pretty sure he's way in over his head!"

Jaz smiled but didn't say anything. She was determined not to give away the surprise. Jonathan had invited her and Maria over to his house last week to double check that everything was wheelchair accessible for both Maria and Carrie's mom. He'd done well with everything except the transition to the back yard deck, and he assured Maria he'd have that fixed before the party. Even the main floor bathroom was accessible with a grab bar, a taller toilet and lots of room to turn around in a wheelchair. She didn't know why he was working so hard to make his house accessible, but it sure was a thoughtful thing to do.

"Here, let's go in the backyard to visit after we all change out of our party clothes." Carrie interrupted Jaz's thoughts and turned to the stairs. "Katie, can you bring out drinks for you kids and Jaz? And I'll finish my coffee." She came back downstairs a minute later in her shorts and t-shirt, sank into one of the lawn chairs in the backyard, and stretched out her legs. "I don't ever want to see a book or a computer screen again!"

"Sounds like it was pretty brutal."

Carrie nodded, "If I knew how hard getting my master's would be, I honestly wouldn't have done it. The whole past eight months is a total blur. It's a miracle the kids survived. Well, actually, it's probably all due to Jonathan. He even started having the kids spend the weekends at his house so I could focus on studying. Without his help I don't know what I would have done."

"So, you're glad you finally agreed to date him?" Jaz smirked, remembering how hard Carrie tried to resist falling for him.

She reached out and playfully smacked Jaz's leg. "Yeah-yeah, you were right miss know-it-all. After having Matthew and Katie it's the best thing I've ever done."

Jaz grasped her throat in mock horror, "Better than letting some lost preggo chick invade your house? I'm shocked!" She turned and accepted the glass of lemonade that Katie brought over to her. "Thanks girl!"

"Well, maybe best thing *after* letting you in. Maybe. So tell me, how's the business going?"

"Crazy good! Mostly thanks to Maria, Lisa, and Lauren. They've been helping me scale the business and expand—just like you've done with *Framed*. Maria's officially been my Executive Assistant for a while now, and I pay her a salary and everything. And Lisa's finally quit her job so starting the beginning of May she'll work part-time doing all the finances for the business, and part-time with her free-lance clients. And every time I get overwhelmed with the whole mom thing I text Lauren and she calms me down."

"Wow! It's like I've been away for years and I've missed everything! And how are you balancing running a business with having a baby?"

"It's been OK. Harder, for sure, but I'm learning to get more people to help with the things I don't need to be doing. I have five women working as sub-contractors, and they do almost all the sewing for me. So that frees me up to do the shopping for more clothes and plan all the designs. And once Lisa's taking care of all the finances I'm going to add a line of accessible clothes for people like Maria—and your mom I guess."

"No way! Oh Jaz, you're amazing!"

"What's accessible mean Mommy?" Katie had been sitting on the grass eating a popsicle and listening carefully.

"Well, in this case it means easy-to-put-on, but specially for people that have a harder time doing things. Like special clothes for Grandma that work with being in a wheelchair."

"Oooohhh. Don't they make those now? Grandma wears clothes every day!"

"There are accessible clothes available," Jaz explained, "But they're not very special. And people like your Grandma and Maria should feel special in their clothes all the time."

"That's good Princess Jasmine. You fix the clothes so Grandma and Maria are princesses *every day*!"

"I'll do my best!" she promised.

CHAPTER 30

That night everyone was dressed in their best outfits to celebrate Carrie's graduation. Jaz was wearing a short black fitted skirt with black strappy sandals and a white blouse that had a single mid-length sleeve and was cut away at an angle on the opposite side. Her only color was turquoise and silver earrings that almost brushed her shoulders. She loved dressing other people in bright colors, but found that she felt best in versions of clothes in black and white.

Alex was looking adorable in little brown shorts, a red plaid button-up shirt, and a blue bandana-style bib with a red bow tie sewed on it. Lisa was wearing a bright yellow wrap dress and high heeled yellow shoes that Jaz found online. The bright colors matched her sunny personality.

Maria was in a long flowery skirt with a white blouse that Jaz had changed up by replacing the long sleeves with lace cap sleeves, and a colorful infinity scarf Jaz repurposed from a vintage silk muumuu.

Carla wore a pair of tan cigarette pants with four pink silk-covered buttons down each side at the hem, and a pink sleeveless top with a scoop next. Chris wore one of Jaz's trademark men's dress shirts with bright accents at the collar, cuffs, and button panel, but he insisted on wearing a pair of dark jeans—no dress pants for him!

Becky was a special challenge for Jaz until she came across a mint green ladies' robe made of the softest jersey material. She turned it into a t-shirt dress for Becky with matching shorts underneath, and then added a little white infinity scarf repurposed from a tablecloth with tassels. Becky loved the feeling of the tassels and the outfit was her new favorite.

Jonathan and his sister-in-law Jenny had decorated the backyard with orange streamers and lanterns that fluttered and sparkled in the evening light. There were fairy lights strung across the yard, and larger strands of vintage-style bulbs around the deck area. Jaz was impressed with how easy it was to push Maria's wheelchair through the house and into the back yard.

Carrie's parents were already there, having arrived just before dinner and thoroughly surprised Carrie and the kids. Jaz thought Jonathan looked a bit nervous. She was sure he'd met Carrie's parents before, but maybe since his own parents had died in a car accident he felt weird around his girlfriend's parents. Carrie, on the other hand, still looked tired, but was glowing as she came to greet everyone.

"If Jaz hadn't dressed us up earlier today I'd say you guys were way over the top. But it looks like our favorite fashion designer has covered all her bases." She hugged everyone and made sure to give Maria and Jaz a special thank you for picking such a nice hotel. "Dad and Mom don't really get to take vacations, and that place makes this weekend extra-special."

"Oh, it was fun! Jaz and I had a lovely afternoon checking out all the fancy hotels. We even had lunch at the one your parents are staying at!"

Carrie grabbed Alex and sent Jaz off to get food, "Jonathan and Jenny seemed to think the whole neighborhood was coming over to eat. Make sure you go back for seconds!"

The party took a bit of a turn when Jenny's parents surprised everyone by coming through the door. Jaz knew that Jenny's husband Max was Jonathan's brother, and that her parents had become substitute parents to both Max and Jonathan when their parents died. But it didn't really make sense for them to fly down for Carrie's graduation. Or for it to be a surprise.

It wasn't until they all gathered in the backyard after eating, and Carrie was thanking everyone that Jaz finally clued in. Standing under a rose arbor that was lit up by fairy lights, Jonathan kneeled on one knee and proposed to Carrie. It was such a touching and happy scene that everyone ended up laughing and crying at the same time. Jaz was sitting back from everyone so she could nurse Alex, and it gave her an opportunity to take everything in. She watched how Carrie went straight to her mom after accepting Jonathan's proposal, and how her parents embraced the kids and Jonathan with such happy faces.

Jaz felt a deep ache in her heart that was physically painful. She had parents, and Alex had grandparents, but their continuing refusal to acknowledge either one of them was hurting more as time went by, rather than less. She wondered if she should just show up on her parents' doorstep and force them to hold Alex. They couldn't possibly say no to him in person, could they?

But that was just the thing. They had already rejected him. And as much as Jaz desperately wanted to have her parents in her life and Alex's, she wasn't willing to risk hurting him in the process. Because the only thing more painful than not having grandparents was having grandparents who didn't want you.

CHAPTER 31

"*J*az? You sure have been quiet lately. What's wrong?" Maria and Jaz were supposed to be going over client bookings while Alex had his afternoon nap.

Jaz felt the tears start to come, and brushed them away. It frustrated her that the pain she felt watching Carrie with her parents was just as sharp today.

"Come on sweetie. I might not be able to fix it, but you can't hold it all in anymore." Maria reached up and cupped Jaz's cheek in her hand.

"At Carrie's party I was watching her with her parents, and watching her kids with their grandparents…" Jaz found herself crying too hard to continue. Maria rubbed her back and gave her time to cry.

"It's terribly unfair that Alex doesn't know his grandparents, isn't it?"

Jaz nodded.

"I don't know what the answer is. Maybe it's time to confront them?"

"I was wondering the same thing." Jaz sniffed and wiped her face,

"But what if they slam the door in Alex's face? I don't want him to be rejected too!"

"Let yourself think of all the options, and just go with whatever seems like the best thing to do. I wish I could tell you what that is, but I just don't know. Whatever happens, we're here for you and Alex."

"I know. Thank you." She reached over and hugged Maria. "OK, let's try and get this new booking schedule figured out..."

The solution to Jaz's hurting heart lay with Maria, but not in a way any of them were expecting. It was a few days later, and she was having trouble walking. "I'm off to get Becky from the bus," she called up to Jaz.

"Are you sure you don't want me to get her? At least take your walker!"

"It's not that far. I'll be OK." But when Maria hadn't come back in the door with Becky a few minutes later, Jaz got worried and went out to check. At first she didn't see anything, so she walked to the end of the pathway to get a look around the shrubs that bordered the property. Maria was lying crumpled on the sidewalk, and Becky was on her knees beside her rocking back and forth.

"Maria! Are you OK?" Jaz cried out as she ran over. She could see right away that something was wrong with Maria's ankle.

"Oh, Jaz, thank goodness! I'm afraid I've really messed things up. I started to lose my balance and tried to avoid falling on Becky, and somehow twisted my ankle."

Jaz reached out her hand for Becky to hold—she knew Becky didn't like hugs, but was obviously quite upset—and tried to remember what she had been taught in first aid. "Um, does anything else hurt?"

"Besides my pride? No. If you help me I can sit up."

"Wait. Are you sure? Your neck or head or anything?"

"I'm sure."

Carefully Jaz helped Maria sit up. It felt a lot better to see her sitting rather than laying on the sidewalk. Becky stopped rocking and stroked Maria's face as she winced. "Oh dear. That's a lot of pain."

"Maria, I have to call the ambulance. You need to get that x-rayed and I can't take you with Alex and Becky."

"Alex! Is he OK?"

"Yeah, he's in his bouncy seat on the floor in the sewing room." Jaz pulled out her phone from her back pocket and dialed 9-1-1. After ringing for a few seconds she was able to ask for an ambulance. But then she didn't know what to do. She didn't want to leave Alex alone in the house, but she didn't want to leave Maria alone on the sidewalk, and Becky still looked very upset. *Think! Think!*

The voice of the 9-1-1 operator broke through her thoughts. "Ma'am? It's going to be about fifteen or twenty minutes. Is your friend in a safe place?"

"I guess. She's on the sidewalk. But it's a pretty quiet road."

"And do you have any way of protecting her from the sun? It can get uncomfortable."

"Oh, well yeah. I can go get an umbrella."

"Alright. Do your best to make her comfortable and please call us back if anything changes, OK?"

Jaz agreed and hung up. "OK, so I need to get you something to keep the sun off. How about I leave you my phone and I'll take Becky with me to go get an umbrella and put Alex in the stroller? And then we'll be right back. Is that alright?"

"Yes, of course. I think Becky should try to go to the bathroom. Do that first. She'll need some help getting her shorts down, and then back up again when she's done. And you wash your hands after Becky, OK?" Becky nodded.

Jaz tried not to let her hand shake as she walked with Becky into the house. In the bathroom, Becky did her best, and Jaz helped when she needed it. Maria always took care of Becky's bathroom needs, so this was all new to Jaz. She hoped she didn't embarrass Becky, or do anything wrong.

After washing their hands, Jaz went upstairs and got Alex who smiled at her brightly, through teary eyes. She had no idea how long he'd been crying, or when he stopped. "Hey you," she tried to say brightly, "We're going to go hang out with Maria on the sidewalk!"

She went back downstairs with him, and found Becky wrist deep in a box of cookies. "Um, maybe just two cookies, OK Becky?"

Becky pulled out two handfuls and Jaz left it. At least the cookies would keep her occupied. She got Alex into the stroller and grabbed an umbrella. Just as she was about to go back out she ran into Maria's room and grabbed all her pillows. "Here Becky, you carry this one, and I'll get the rest." Then she ran back in again, and grabbed an ice pack and a towel from the kitchen.

Awkwardly they made their way back to Maria. Jaz breathed a sigh of relief to see her still looking alive. She gently set the ice pack on the ankle that was already swollen and turning colors.

"Alright, let's try and get these pillows behind you so you can lean back." It took a few tries, until Jaz sat herself back-to-back with a pillow between her and Maria.

"Ah, that helps already. Thank you."

"How's the ankle?"

"Ohhhh… it's still attached."

"Haha." Alex started to fuss, and Jaz had to get up and take him out of the stroller before settling herself down again as Maria's backrest. Then she remembered the umbrella, got up again, and opened up the umbrella before sitting down. Becky finished her cookies and sat down beside Jaz to stroke Alex's cheek. She brought some cookie crumbs with her too that Jaz kept brushing off.

"You know Becky, now would be the perfect time to break out a distracting stream of conversation!"

Becky laughed at Jaz, and reached up to touch her hair. They sat like that until Jaz finally saw the ambulance turn down their road. "Oh, thank God. The ambulance is here Maria." She waved the umbrella in the air, but it wasn't hard for paramedics to spot the strange group of people on the sidewalk. Jaz waited to get up until she knew Maria was well supported. It was a huge relief to suddenly not be the one in charge.

Fifteen minutes later they loaded Maria into the ambulance for a trip to the hospital. Jaz had to keep a tight grip on Becky, who tried to go with Maria. "Where are you taking her?"

"We'll be at St. Vincent's."

"I know where that is Maria, Mom works there. I'll send Lisa over and stay here with Becky." Maria waved a hand in agreement and then they closed the doors and drove away.

"Come on Becky. Let's go in and wait for Daddy to come home." Becky seemed torn between trying to follow the ambulance with Maria, and staying home for Daddy. Finally she decided to follow Jaz, but Jaz made sure to keep a good grip on her hand, just in case she tried to dash off. After a tricky maneuver to get them all inside, she locked the door behind her.

"Alright, I think we're OK now. Becky, let's go find a TV show." Jaz went to put on the kids' channel and waited for Becky to sit down and start watching. Then she went to see to Alex who was in serious need of a diaper change and a feed. Running upstairs she grabbed everything she needed and brought it to the living room so she could keep an eye on Becky.

It wasn't until she was nursing him that she realized she hadn't phoned Lisa yet. Quickly dialing the office, she waited to be put through to Lisa.

"Hey Lisa? Sorry to bother you at work, but your Mom's had a fall and I think she broke her ankle."

"Oh my gosh! Where is she?"

"The ambulance just left to take her to St. Vincent's. It's only her ankle, everything else is fine. Um, I was going to stay here with Becky and Alex until Chris comes home. Can you go to the hospital? I forgot to grab her purse or anything."

"You have Becky too? Shoot! Should I get Carrie to come over?"

"No, I think we're OK. She went to the bathroom, and had a bunch of cookies, and now she's watching TV."

"Alright. Well it sounds like you've got everything under control. I'll get a taxi to the hospital right away, and then can you bring her purse whenever you can come? I think Chris should be home soon."

"Yeah, of course."

Jaz hung up and rested her head against the back of the chair. She should have insisted Maria let her get Becky! It was getting harder for her to walk, and Jaz *knew* she had been in pain all day. By the time Chris got home, Jaz gave a fast explanation and then grabbed everything and left with Alex for the hospital.

CHAPTER 32

"*M*rs. Naylor? Maria Naylor?"

"Yes, over here!" Maria waved from her wheelchair where she was waiting for an x-ray. Lisa had just found her a few minutes ago, and Maria was quite embarrassed to tell her how silly she had been to insist on going without her walker to get Becky. Lisa got up to wheel Maria in, but the x-ray technician reached for the wheelchair.

"I'll take her in, and then bring her back here after the x-rays."

"OK, see you soon Mom."

"Bye dear."

"That's your daughter?" the lady asked as she wheeled Maria into the x-ray room.

"Yep, my only daughter. She's a bookkeeper at Golden Lion Investments for another few days, and then she'll be working full-time for our friend's business."

"That sounds nice. Now, I'm going to need you to get up on the table, but we'll take it nice and slow."

"Alright. It was my silly stumbling that got me into this mess, so I'll try not to fall again."

"I'll give you all the support you need Mrs. Naylor."

"Oh, please call me Maria. And what's your name?"

"I'm Allison. Allison Lee."

"Oh, are you related to Jasmine Lee?"

The lady jerked around and stared at Maria with her mouth open. For a second she looked near tears, then she tightened her jaw. "Nope, don't know her."

In that second Maria felt like her fall had a divine purpose. *Of course* she was Jaz's mom! Who else could it be? She said a quick prayer and started talking. "That's too bad. Jaz is lovely. She lives with my daughter and I! Such a smart girl. And her business? She's on her way to fame for sure, and she's so nice about how she treats everyone."

"Mrs. Naylor, I need you to lay down and be very still."

"Maria, call me Maria." She smiled at Jaz's mom and tried to make eye contact but Allison was having none of that. She quickly bustled out of the room to take the first x-ray. As soon as she came back Maria was ready for her.

"And her little boy? Oh my goodness. I thought my baby was the most beautiful baby in the world, but little Alexander Stanley takes the cake for sure!"

"What did you say?"

"Oh, takes the cake. I guess that's a strange expre—"

"No, what did you say his name was?"

"Alexander Stanley. Jaz said he had to have his grandfather's name. Like I was saying, such a beautiful baby. Really a model for Asian genetics!"

"He's Asian?"

"100 percent! And Jaz dresses him so smartly! Always a perfect outfit on that little guy! It's a shame his family hasn't met him yet."

"Where's the father?"

"That's the sad part. Can you believe he begged Jaz not to tell his parents? And she didn't! Honored his request, and now she's supporting that little boy and raising him all on her own. We wanted to give her a break on rent—you know teenage mom and all that—but she more than pays her own way. I told you how smart she was, didn't I? Very smart. Lovely girl."

Maria paused and looked at Allison. Carefully she put her hand on her arm. "I lost my daughter for four years because I was too afraid to stand up to my husband. Four years. But when I had nowhere else to turn, Lisa came back and forgave me. My life is so full now, but I'll always regret the time I lost."

The silence hung heavy in the darkened room. Finally, Allison took a big shuddering breath. "I need to have you turn your knee in as best you can for the next x-ray."

Maria followed her instructions quietly, trying to figure out what to do next. But she didn't want to push too hard. When the x-rays were done, she was helped into the wheelchair and slowly wheeled back towards the waiting room. Maria's sharp eyes immediately picked up Jaz with Alex, sitting beside Lisa. She held up her hand and waved Allison down to her.

"That's her there. Jaz and baby Alex. It's OK if it's too much for you now. But please don't wait much longer. Jaz misses you and her daddy terribly and she wants you to know your grandson."

Allison looked over to Jaz for a minute before turning to Maria with tears in her eyes. "I'm sorry," she whispered. "I can't." She turned and slipped out, and Maria wheeled herself back to her favorite people.

"Hey, you've got to wheel yourself around now?" Lisa protested.

"Ah, she was busy with the next patient. We can go back to the emergency room now and wait for the results."

They did their best to keep things cheerful while they waited, and Jaz ended up taking Alex over to another lady who kept smiling and waving at him. She sat on the edge of the bed and propped up Alex where the lady could touch him. Her eyes lit up.

Maria turned to Lisa, and caught a glimpse of Jaz's mom, almost hidden from view, watching her daughter and grandson. She looked sad and uncertain. They were all interrupted by the doctor arriving, and Jaz quickly made her way back to Maria after letting the lady give Alex a little kiss on his cheek. He was gurgling happily with all the attention he was getting in this strange, bright place.

When Maria looked up again, Allison was gone.

Another hour to get a cast on, and they were on their way home. Jaz drove and Lisa called in a pizza order for delivery.

"Girls, I am so sorry I was too proud to take the walker to get Becky. Jaz, you told me, and I just didn't listen. And now you're stuck with an invalid."

"Aw, don't worry Mom! You were practically an invalid already. Now you're just a bigger one!"

They all laughed, and the last of the tension from the day left everyone. Later after they had all gone to bed, Maria lay awake and wondered what to do next.

CHAPTER 33

*J*az woke up the next morning to the sounds of Alex fussing. He was sleeping through the night most of the time now, but that meant that he often woke up demanding his breakfast. She quickly changed him and then settled back on her bed to nurse. He looked up at her with such trusting eyes. "I love you Alex," she whispered and was rewarded with a full on smile before he went back to his breakfast.

She reached over and grabbed her phone. It was fun to start her morning watching the online sales confirmations come in. But this morning there was something totally different.

Jasmine, this is your mom. I do not know if you still have this number. Text me back if you do.

Jaz's first thought was that something bad had happened to her dad. Why else would her mom just text her out of the blue. Quickly she answered.

Mommy, yes this is still my number. Are you OK? Is Daddy OK?

She hit send and held her breath, waiting for an answer.

We are fine. How are you?

Again, Jaz found tears falling down her cheeks, but this time they were tears of happiness and hope.

I'm really good. But I miss you so much. And I'm so, so sorry for disappointing you.

The next response shocked Jaz.

Can we see you? Today?

Alex finished just as Jaz was about to respond, and she gently sat him up for a burp. *Was it possible? Could her parents actually forgive her? Would Alex finally meet his grandparents?* Setting him back on the bed between her legs she sent her response.

Yes! I'm free this morning. Do you want to come here? The address is 17 Pinetree Cres, just a few minutes from you.

Yes, we will be there at 10.

"Maria! Lisa!" Jaz hollered as she grabbed Alex and ran out of the room.

"What? What's wrong?" Lisa walked out of her room tying her robe.

"Quick! Let's go downstairs!" she jogged down the stairs with Alex laughing at the bumps and burst into Maria's room. "Maria! My mom and dad are coming to see me! Today! This morning!"

"Oh, Jaz, that's wonderful! I met your mom yesterday you know."

"What? No way? Why didn't you tell me?"

"Come on you three. Sit on my bed and I'll tell you what happened."

She told them about her conversation with Allison, and then about seeing her watching Jaz and Alex in the emergency room.

"I can't believe it," Jaz shook her head, "Do you think they'll actually want to forgive me?"

"Let's hope for the best, shall we?" Maria reached over and grabbed Jaz's hand, "And remember, no matter what, we're here for you!"

Jaz left the room so Lisa could help Maria get to the bathroom. She chose their outfits for the day carefully. Alex was dressed in the same outfit he wore to Carrie's graduation party, and Jaz put on one of the dresses she had made from a navy blue men's dress shirt. It was accented with a thin orange fabric belt, and orange piping around the collar. She slipped on a pair of orange sandals, completing the outfit. With a big breath, she went down to get ready for meeting her parents.

"Do you want us to be here when your parents come?"

Jaz looked up from the table at Lisa who was making breakfast for everyone. It had become one of their traditions to have a nice breakfast together on Saturdays. "Yeah, definitely. It's such a weird feeling. I'm not nervous really, but I am. I want them to love Alex and forgive me...but I don't want to have this huge expectation."

Maria joined them, slowly wheeling herself to the table and reached across to hug Jaz when she moved a chair to make space for her. "I think this is a good thing. It might take a while for you all to get used to each other—and I suspect your parents will have a hard time thinking of you as a grown woman instead of their little girl—but it's going to be OK."

"I hope you're right."

Lisa brought up some questions about the business and Jaz gratefully followed the topic change. Carla and Becky came up to check on Maria, and Jaz and Lisa cleaned up the dishes. Becky clearly didn't like the wheelchair, until Jaz went and got Alex from his bouncy chair and set him on Maria's lap.

"See Becky? Alex doesn't mind the wheelchair. It's still Maria, just in a funny chair!"

Becky looked at Jaz sideways for a few seconds before slowing walking over and stroking Alex's head. He rewarded her with a huge gummy smile. She smiled back and leaned her head on Maria's shoulder.

"Thank you," Carla said, "You're really getting good with her! And I can't imagine how you handled everything yesterday on your own! Chris said you had everything under control when he got home."

"Well, we'll see how today goes."

"What do you mean?"

"It's the weirdest thing. Maria's x-ray tech yesterday turned out to be my mom."

"No!" Carla gasped.

"Yep, and now my parents are coming over for a visit. My mom texted this morning. They'll be here at ten."

"Oh, Jaz," she walked over with tears in her eyes and gave her a hug, "I hope this works out. I know how much you've missed them."

"Thanks." Jaz felt her own eyes welling up. "I'll have to try to keep a grip on my emotions when they come. My mom's not exactly the crying type."

"You just be you, however that looks! But I think this guy might need some freshening up before they come!" Maria looked at Jaz with a twinkle in her eye, and when Jaz picked up Alex Becky grunted and started waving her hands in front of her nose. Her reaction had everyone laughing.

"Well, we'll be downstairs or in the backyard if you need anything. I'll say a prayer that it all goes well."

"Thanks Carla! Bye Becky!"

The doorbell rang just as Jaz was coming back down the stairs with Alex. She took a deep breath, and then opened the door to her parents. She managed to squeak out, "Mommy, Daddy…" and then felt paralyzed. Her parents looked different. Tired. Older. Her dad had some new streaks of grey in his carefully styled hair, and his white dress shirt and navy dress pants looked a little too big on him. Her mom was wearing navy capris and a white polo shirt with the right logo embroidered onto it. Jaz realized with a start that her mom's hairstyle was almost identical to her own but with longer bangs.

"Ah, there's my favorite x-ray technician! So nice to see you again Allison! And you must be Stanley. I'm Maria. Come in! Come in!" Maria wheeled herself right to them and reached out her hand. They both shook her hand silently as they stepped into the house.

"Um, do you want to go to the living room?"

Taking off their shoes, they followed Jaz into the living room. Alex's bright eyes looked carefully at the new faces in his life.

"This is Lisa, Maria's daughter." Lisa stood up from the armchair and shook both their hands before gesturing to them to sit down. Jaz sat on the edge of the couch beside her dad and turned Alex around to sit facing out. He gazed at his grandpa beside him before trying to look up at his mom. She bent over and kissed the top of his head. "And, um, this is Alex. Alexander Stanley Lee."

Her dad reached over with a shaking hand and touched the top of Alex's hand. Immediately the baby grasped it. With his other hand her dad wiped a tear from the corner of his eye. They all sat there, as if suspended in time.

"Would you like to hold him Daddy?"

He nodded and Jaz put her son into his grandpa's lap for the first time. The tears were falling freely now. "He's perfect," he whispered.

"When was he born?" her mom's voice seemed brash and loud.

"Oh, um, February eighth. In the morning."

Alex was suddenly interested in this new voice. He looked up at his grandma for a minute, and then gave her a smile. She reached out towards his foot and then jerked her hand back.

"It is not right that you got pregnant Jasmine." She wouldn't even look directly at Jaz, although her gaze kept slipping over to Alex.

"I know Mommy. But now I'm here, and so is Alex. And that won't change." She tried to keep her voice gentle, but firm. Like Carrie taught her. It was time to speak up for what was important in her world. "He's a very good baby, and I'm doing OK as his mom."

"More than OK," Maria reminded her, and then turned to Jaz's parents, "Yesterday, when I fell, Jaz was amazing. I was outside picking up Becky from the bus—that's the little girl who lives downstairs with her parents—and I fell. I didn't even have my phone on me to call for help but as soon as Jaz realized I wasn't back at the right time she came and checked on me. She took care of me, Becky, and Alex without batting an eye."

Jaz smiled her thanks at Maria, and her dad reached over and patted her on the knee. It was the first contact she had with him in almost a year, and the feeling inside made her almost whimper. He cleared his throat.

"Your mom... we... there's things you need to know." Beside him, her mom visibly stiffened.

"Stanley," she warned, glancing at Maria and Lisa.

"You know," started Maria, "I need to get my foot up for a while. And Lisa was just heading out to get some groceries. We'll leave you four alone." She smiled at the couple, "It was lovely to meet you. Come on over any time. We like a busy household here!"

Lisa stood up and said good-bye before wheeling Maria to her bedroom. A few minutes later the front door quietly closed.

Jaz's dad scooted back on the couch so Jaz could see her mom. Jaz didn't know what to do except wait for one of them to start talking.

"Your father was very bad when he was younger. Very bad. His mom did not control him, and he got a girl pregnant."

Jaz felt her world tilt unexpectedly. She suddenly had a thousand questions, but the hard look on her mom's face stopped her. *Why was her mom telling her all of this? Didn't she want to know about Jaz and Alex? The past didn't matter, did it?*

"Her parents were very angry. They were going to put the baby up for adoption but your father would not allow it. He insisted that he could raise the baby, even though he still had two years of university left." She looked down at her hands, which were constantly twisting, "My parents wanted to arrange a marriage for me in China with a very bad man. He was willing to pay and they were very poor…"

Seeing her mom's chin begin to tremble Jaz got up and kneeled on the floor beside her mom. She reached out to hold her hands, but her mom jerked them away. "Everyone knew about the pregnant girl who had shamed her family, and the boy who thought he could raise a baby on his own…" The air seemed to leave her body and she sank back on the couch.

Her dad took up the story, "Your mom offered me a solution that would help both of us. We could get married and move to a new city as soon as you were born. We would claim you belonged to both of us. She would continue to work at the hospital and I would raise you…"

The air was heavy with tension and unspoken words. Alex began to fuss, and Jaz stood up and took him. Snuggling him into her body she began to pace back and forth, trying to ignore the truth that was staring her in the face.

"You're not… you didn't…"

"I am not your real mom Jasmine."

CHAPTER 34

*J*az sat down hard in the armchair. The sudden movement startled Alex and he began to cry. Without thinking she began to nurse him, and then saw the looks on her parent's faces. She reached down and grabbed a baby blanket from the basket on the floor and covered herself.

She didn't know what was more shocking. Her mom actually opening up to her, or what she said. Jaz tried to sort out the confusion in her head. Suddenly, she remembered something Carrie had said after the terrible incident with her ex-husband. *You can't change the past, so focusing on it too much is pointless. What really matters is what you choose to do next.*

"Did you love me? *Do* you love me?"

"I tried to do my best for you."

"That doesn't answer my question."

Her dad leaned forward, his arms on his knees, "Your mother and I love you very much. We wanted you to have everything we never had."

"Mommy?"

"You don't have to call me that anymore."

Alex murmured and made some noisy smacking sounds from under the blanket. The interruption was so unexpected Jaz smiled. She thought back to Maria and Lisa's story before answering her mom.

"I don't have to, but I want to. You *are* my mom. You raised me as your daughter. It doesn't matter whose belly I came from."

"Do you really think that Jasmine?"

"I do."

Now it was her mom's turn to get emotional. A single tear escaped and rolled down her cheek. "I tried to raise you right. I was there when you were born. They treated her so badly, even when she was in labor. Like she was a curse. I did not want that for you."

"But that's exactly what you did to me."

Her mom looked down at her still-twisting hands. "Yes," she whispered.

Clearing his throat, her dad tried to speak. "Could you..."

"I want Alex to know his grandparents. I want... I wish I could call you up. And visit. But I'm really different now. You have to be OK with that. I don't think I'll ever go to university. And I definitely won't become a surgeon or a lawyer." She smiled gently at her mom, "And I'll be keeping my hair like this. Like yours."

"Oh Jasmine. I will try to be OK with that. But this is not what we chose for you. You are giving up so much. And our friends..."

"Mom. Friends should be the people that don't care if you screw up. Or if your kids screw up. Friends don't care about stuff like that. They're just your friends. I'm done trying to be anyone other than myself." Now she smiled brightly, "You need to be friends with Maria! She's awesome, and she already likes me!"

"All these white people around you…"

"Mom, they don't see me as different. And if you see them as people just like you, you'll be happy."

Her dad cleared his throat again, "That's just what we want for you."

Alex was now sleeping peacefully. Jaz adjusted her clothes and then carefully got up, "I'm going to put him in his crib now. Do you want to see my room?" They nodded and followed her upstairs. After Jaz lay Alex down her mom walked over to the crib and lay her hand on his head for a moment. Then they all slipped out of the room and Jaz closed the door behind them.

"Um, would you like to see what I do?"

Again they both nodded and Jaz led them into her sewing room. She showed them the jean jacket she was working on, as well as the closet and shelf full of finished products. "And over here is where I put the online orders that came in overnight—I haven't had a chance to do that yet this morning. They go down to Maria who takes care of printing the labels, and then Carla from downstairs picks them up each evening and packs them to take to the post office first thing tomorrow."

"And these people do this for free?"

"Oh, gosh no! I pay them all! Maria is my Executive Assistant, so she gets paid the most. Carla gets paid per order. Oh, the ladies that do the sewing, they get paid every Friday when they bring in the finished projects and pick up next week's work. The only person who's been helping for free is Lisa. She's been helping me with the bookkeeping. But Tuesday is her last day at her corporate job, and then she'll be on a salary too. I can't wait to have her help every day. Sometimes I spend all day doing other things besides sewing and…" She suddenly paused, aware that she was rambling. Her parents had always raised her to answer direct questions and then be quiet. "I'm sorry. I get a little excited about everything."

"It is going to take some time to get used to this Jasmine. It is not what we planned for you—" Her mom seemed trapped between wanting to walk away and wanting to stay.

"—But we're very happy for you." her dad added.

They all stood there in silence. "So... what's next? Do you want to come and see Alex again soon? Or...?"

Her parents looked at each other, silent communication shared with glances that Jaz couldn't interpret. "Would you like to come over for lunch next Sunday?" her mom asked.

"Um, yeah. Yes. Thank you."

"We'll see you next Sunday then," her dad added. They made their way back downstairs and said goodbye. Jaz noticed they had walked over. She couldn't think of a time when her dad had walked instead of driving his Lexus LS. After closing the door quietly she walked over and tapped on Maria's door.

"Come in!" Maria was sitting up in bed, reading a novel. Popping a bookmark in, she patted the bed beside her and Jaz sat down. "Well, it sounds like that went quite well!"

"Yeah, I think so. But you're never going to believe what they told me!"

"What?"

"I'm still trying to grasp it myself. But the thing is, my dad's my real dad but my mom's not my real mom."

"What?" The front door opened and they heard Lisa coming in.

"Hang on..." Jaz went out to help Lisa with the groceries. "You gotta come hear this, "she said as soon as the frozen and fridge stuff were put away. Lisa followed her back into Maria's bedroom.

"OK. So the thing is, my dad's my real dad but my mom's not my real mom."

Lisa's eyes bugged out. "What?"

"That's exactly what I said! Even hearing it twice doesn't make any more sense."

"I'll try and get it straight. My dad got someone pregnant in university. Her parents tried to force her to have it adopted but he refused and insisted on raising the baby—me! And then somehow in there my mom—my mom now—was about to have to go to China to marry some guy but instead she asked my dad to marry her and they moved here. And never told me any of this until today."

"That is just…" Lisa couldn't find the words to explain her feelings about what she heard.

"Bizarre?" Jaz offered.

"Kind of. But that doesn't explain why your mom reacted so strongly to your pregnancy. I mean, you'd think she would've been more sympathetic."

"I think she was determined to raise me 'right' because she didn't want me to go through what my biological mom went through from her family. I did tell her she had pretty much done the same thing. She didn't actually apologize, but I don't think she's as angry at me anymore."

"So, what happens next?"

"They invited Alex and I over for lunch next Sunday. I did think maybe they'd want to see him again sooner, but it's better than nothing. I actually have a ton of questions for them, but I don't want to push things. My mom seemed… hard and fragile at the same time."

"And you still think of her as your mom?"

"Definitely. She raised me. And she even said something about being there when I was born. Like I said, *lots* of questions."

"Well, those will all be answered in due time I'm sure. And although I still feel quite silly for my fall, I think we can say it helped things turn in a better direction for you!"

"Yeah, but no more falls, OK? I prefer you in one piece." Jaz reached over and hugged Maria, "And thank you, for connecting with my mom and making this all happen."

"You're welcome! Now, I think we barely have time for lunch before clients start coming."

"Right. I kinda forgot about all that. I'm just going to get the orders ready for you and then I'll come back down."

"Oh, and it might be nice to send your mom a little thank you text for her visit."

"I'll do that right away!"

CHAPTER 35

A message came through overnight.

Heyyyy Jaz! Long time no chat! I heard you were back in town. Wanna meet at Connie's today?

Jaz stared at her phone in confusion for a minute before making the connection. Sherry. One of her old 'best' friends who had called a teenage mom a slut the last time Jaz had spent time at the lake. She sighed and turned off her phone. No need to deal with that right now. It was Friday morning, and with five contractors coming over with new projects to check, new instructions to give, and payments to make, Jaz had enough on her plate.

She looked down at Alex who was nursing and staring up at her with his big brown trusting eyes. "You will never use language like that. And you will always know that everyone has a story and deserves a chance." He stopped drinking long enough to coo back at her. She stroked his hair and smiled. There was just enough dark brown hair for her to brush it to the side, and it made him look even cuter. "I love you."

The day flew by. But in the back of her mind, Jaz kept thinking about her morning text. There was a part of her that missed hanging out with friends her own age. She thought back to a year ago when she was still hoping she wasn't pregnant. Things could have turned out so differently.

At suppertime she brought up Sherry's text.

"What do you think I should do?"

"Well, it sure would be nice for you to have some friends your own age!" Maria always thought the best of people.

"Yeah, but why would her friend just text out of the blue. If she was a real friend, she would have tried to keep in touch with Jaz last year."

"I did uninstall the app we all used to chat last year when I found out they all thought I took a gap year…"

"Did you change your number or block them?"

"No…" Jaz could see where Lisa was going with this. "And you're right. None of them tried to text or call me. But maybe things are different now."

After Alex was sleeping for the night she texted Sherry back.

> *Hi! Yeah. It's been a while. I could meet at Connie's tomorrow around 11 if you're still interested. You do know I have a baby, right?*

She hit send before she could change her mind. Alex was the most important person in her life. If he wasn't welcome somewhere, she wasn't going. And if Sherry knew she was 'back in town' this morning, then everyone would know by now. It had to have been her mom who told one of the other moms. Jaz wondered what she said. She determined to ask her on Sunday when she had lunch at her parents.

I know! I can't believe you had a baby! That's so cool! OK, see you tomorrow!

Lisa assured Jaz she could use the car in the morning. Already Jaz was planning what Alex and her would wear...

"So I've had time to go over all the numbers for the business." Lisa's voice interrupted her thoughts.

"What? Oh! Great!" She sat down beside her at the table and leaned over to look at Lisa's laptop screen. It was filled with spreadsheets and numbers.

"Do you have any idea what you've been making every month?"

"Not really, no. I mean, I take $1,500 out of the business account every month to pay myself—like you told me. And I pay all the contractors every Friday. Actually, *you* did all the transfers today. Which was *awesome* by the way. How did I do it without you?"

Lisa smiled. Maria muted the TV and piped up from her chair in the living room. "Is it over $5,000 Lisa? I was thinking about this the other day. We're doing at least a hundred every day just with the online orders. And Jaz sees, what, ten clients a week here for sales? Fifteen?"

Lisa smiled even bigger. "I have to admit, going over all the finances for the Jazzy Clothing Company has been the most fun I've ever had bookkeeping. OK, are you ready for some numbers?"

They nodded.

"Let's start with online sales. The average per day for online sales is $130, with postage on top of that. Now, keep in mind, we don't process online orders on the weekend. Carla does them all on Monday. *But* I wanted to know how much per day it was. We pay Carla a per order handling fee of $3. It's an average of three orders per day, so we take her $9 out of the $130, leaving $121 per day."

"I know that sounds good," Jaz was doing the math in her head,

"But that doesn't cover paying the contractors, and the cost of materials."

"Right, I haven't included that. But stick with me here," Again, Lisa couldn't seem to keep the smile off her face.

"So, that's over $3,500 per month. *Just* for the online sales."

"WOOHOO!" Maria called from her chair, and everyone laughed.

"Now, let's look at the rest of your numbers. You actually see up to twenty clients here at the house in any given week. And you sell an average of $75 to each of them. Your highest sale was $325 and your lowest sale was $15."

"I remember both of those! The big sale was this lady who bought Christmas outfits for herself and her family. She was *so* excited for family pictures! And the small sale was a lady who bought a set of bandana bibs for her nephew. She came back after she got paid and bought an outfit for him for $25."

"That's interesting. We don't have any data for repeat customers in person. In the long run, knowing how many people become repeat customers would be helpful."

"Oh, I could do that! All I have to do is go through the appointments! I can tell you though, a lot of them come back at least once every few months."

Jaz turned to look at Maria, "They come back because they love you! I think in marketing guides they call it the 'Maria effect'!"

Lisa was still all business and continued, "Well, if that's the case, she's really helping with sales. Remember, it's an average of $75 in sales *each visit*. Repeat or not."

"Holy cow..." Jaz was starting to see why Lisa was so happy.

"Are you ready for it?"

"Oh, for Pete's sake Lisa! Just tell us the numbers!" Maria wished she had her phone with her so she could use the calculator on it and not be in suspense anymore.

"Six. Thousand. For the in-person sales."

"Wait! So you're saying the business is almost grossing ten thousand a month?"

"Exactly. In fact, this month you'll almost certainly cross the ten thousand mark. And if you keep doing what you're doing, that number will continue to grow. Now," Lisa held up her hand to pause their input, "This has been your steep growth phase. Many businesses have a sharp increase at some point, but then taper off a bit. It would be almost impossible to maintain this rate of growth."

"OK, but how much are we spending a month paying for everything?"

Maria struggled to get up and into her wheelchair and then made her way over to the table. "Now you stop just a minute there young lady!"

"Huh?"

"Before you get all practical, we need to celebrate! Lisa, I think it's prosecco time!"

"Agreed, Mom." She got up and went to the fridge where a bottle had been waiting at the back of the shelf for just such an occasion. "Jaz, you need to celebrate how incredibly successful you are!"

They toasted the Jazzy Clothing Company and each other before getting back to the numbers—although the atmosphere around the table remained quite energetic.

"OK, so let's look at what you're spending. Hang on..." Lisa ran upstairs and came back down with a notebook and pencil. "Let's do this old school." She began to write:

- $3,630 Online Sales
- $6,000 Client Sales

$9,630 TOTAL Income

- $1,500 Jaz Salary
- $1,250 Maria Salary
- $1,000 Lisa Salary
- $270 Carla Shipping/Handling
- $2,500 Contractor Payments
- $800 Clothing/Supplies Purchases

$7,320 TOTAL Expenses

"Wait... so I'm barely clearing $2,000 a month?"

"Wrong. *You* are clearing over $2,000 a month now, and the business has actually been clearing $3,000 a month the last few months. Remember, my salary won't start coming out until the end of this month because I'm just starting."

"What about taxes?" Maria wondered.

"Good question. Jaz, as far as your personal taxes go, you'll probably fall into the 10% category. You're really not taking much for yourself. Actually, maybe you need to talk to Jenny about budgeting and financial planning. Especially now that you have Alex."

"Jenny..." Jaz knew the name was familiar but couldn't place it.

"Carrie's financial planner friend. She's the one who helped Carrie and Lauren get their finances set up. And she has a lot of really high net worth clients that she works with, so she knows her stuff."

"Oh. OK."

"So, where were we..." Lisa continued, "Oh yeah. We've covered your personal taxes. Corporate taxes aren't going to be much more. I've been looking into small business tax rates. You can still claim some more deductions—like part of the rent you pay here—because you use that one room exclusively for your business. I'll look into it more to make sure we're claiming everything we can. But just for now, let's plan for 10% corporate tax as well."

"OK, so the business will clear about $2,000 after taxes starting this month, right?" The elation from a few minutes ago was starting to fade.

"Right. That's *if* you don't do anything different. Jaz, stop and think for a minute. The business is less than a year old. You're paying all three of us, plus *five* contractors, *and* banking money! That's really amazing!"

"Yeah, but if we want to solving housing problems for people like Susan, we're going to need way more money. Way more!" She slumped in her chair, feeling discouraged despite Lisa's encouragement.

"Poor Susan, every time she tries to leave, her daughter finds one more reason to make her stay." Maria often found herself trying to figure out a solution for her friend, but with no luck.

"We can talk about that next, but let's stick to the numbers for now."

Maria and Jaz shared a glance. They often got off track when they were talking about the business. Having Lisa there was going to force them to focus!

"I need to do more research," Lisa continued, "But here's some things we can do. The first is raising the prices. This is an exclusive product and even a 10% increase in price shouldn't deter your customers, but will bring in about another $1,000 per month."

Jaz was nodding, "And with you taking over the finances I'll have time to do more sewing. Which means more listings and more sales. But I really think you two should be paid more. I mean, if you were living on your own there's no way you could pay the bills with what I pay you."

"Well, keep in mind that Mom and I are only part-time workers. So I think the salaries are fair."

"And I really don't even need a salary. All of this is so much fun!"

"No way!" Jaz shook her head. "You are not doing this for free. Remember, you also help out with watching Alex."

Lisa smiled her approval, "Agreed. Now, the other option besides increasing prices is increasing the number of sales. Jaz, that's really on your shoulders to figure out. Things like advertising, finding other channels to sell to... I'm not really sure about that."

"You know, Carrie did a thing a while ago where she got a TV station to do a report on Lauren for their Go Green week. It was all about repurposing stuff and keeping it out of landfills." Jaz pulled out her phone and sent a text to Carrie. "There, I've texted Carrie to see how she got on that show."

"That's a great idea, because it's free promotion. You'd have to plan for it though, because you could get a huge spike in people wanting to buy stuff."

"OK. Well, that would fit with me having more time to sew, and bump up the listings."

Maria topped off their glasses while they continued to talk about different possibilities for growing the business.

"Oh, there's just one more thing before we finish up," Lisa finished her prosecco and smiled. "Gosh, I love these business meetings. Much better than the ones at Golden Lion where they served burnt coffee! Anyways, Jaz, aside from pulling funds for salaries and supplies, you really haven't spent much from your business account. Right now the balance sits at $9,749."

"What?!" Jaz had quit checking her business bank balance at the beginning of the year. She knew there was always money to cover her expenses so she hadn't really thought about it. "That's a *lot* more than I thought it would be. Wow."

"Are you at least paying attention to your personal bank account?" Lisa had a teasing note to her voice, but Jaz knew that she'd follow-up with some advice if she needed to.

"Yes. *That* I've been doing. There's about $1,520 in there, and I've paid the rent and my phone bill for the month. Honestly, except for buying shoes and underwear for me, and diapers and baby gear for Alex, we really don't need much. I think a lot of that is because I live here. If I had to pay for food and utilities and everything there wouldn't be much left."

"You're right." Maria added, "And I think that's why it's hard for people like Susan to move out. It's really hard to make ends meet if you have to pay for everything yourself."

"Why doesn't Susan hook-up with that guy from the library?" Jaz joked, "Then they could split the cost!"

"That's not a bad idea…"

"Lisa, seriously? I was joking!"

"It goes back to my boarding house idea…"

"Your what?"

"When Lisa was a little girl, she dreamed of having her own boarding house. You know, where people pay rent for a room in a house, and eat their meals together."

"That's what we do." Jaz reminded her, "Well, what I do, and sort of what your Airbnb guests do."

"Exactly! That's why it might work!"

"I still don't totally get it."

"What if we bought a house, and set it up like a boarding house? Where people could rent a room and share the costs of the house. Maybe one for older people like Susan and the library guy."

"His name is Martin. You don't have to keep calling him the library guy!"

"Fine, Martin. And maybe we could renovate the living room to be a sewing studio or something. So people like Susan could have a place to work, but still have their private space when they need it!"

"I love it! And if the business was making enough money to cover the monthly costs of the house, then their rent could be way lower!"

"Whoa, I'm not suggesting you put all your profits into this!" Lisa was surprised at Jaz's enthusiasm.

"Why not?"

"Well, because you have your own expenses and future to take care of. One day Alex will be in school and activities. And you'll want to take vacations, buy your own car, buy your own house—we haven't talked about your own long term plans at all, but that stuff all costs money. A lot of money. If you give it all away you'll always struggle to raise Alex."

"Well, I guess the only choice then is to make more money. Let's start by raising the prices by 10%. Maria, can you take care of that over the next few days?"

"Right…" Lisa laughed, "I forgot for a minute I wasn't at a big corporation that had tons of politics to work through, and then regulations. It took us over six months to raise the rent in one of our buildings!"

"I think it's so cool that we're not stuck in that! And I want the business to always be fun, and happy, and flexible."

"You got it boss!"

Everything they had talked about left Jaz feeling too hyped up to try sleeping. Instead, she went into her sewing room and looked around. It would be fun to wear something new to go to Connie's with Alex tomorrow.

She pulled out a bright blue men's t-shirt. The color would look great against Alex's skin, but it was too bright for her. And it was time for some new designs for the cut-out t-shirts. They still sold really well but Jaz was getting tired of the same old phrases. If only there was something special to co-ordinate her outfit with Alex's without being cheesy…

3:16 am. "Holy cow," Jaz whispered. As usual, she was so caught up with sewing she lost track of time. But the finished products were some of her favorites so far. After looking up the Chinese characters for 'momma' and 'baby' she made Alex a little t-shirt from the deep blue shirt, and cut out the characters for 'baby' and backed them with white fabric. Jaz had done something similar for herself, but with a white shirt backed in the bright blue, and the characters for 'momma'. They were more intricate than English letters and took quite a long time to finish them, but she loved the result.

She'd pair her shirt with dark denim capris and white runners, and Alex would wear little denim shorts, and a pair of white baby Nike's that Jaz bought online. No matter what Sherry thought of them, Jaz was excited to go out with her baby in matching outfits.

CHAPTER 36

"*J*az! Over here!" Sherry was already at a table, waving enthusiastically when Jaz wheeled the stroller into Connie's.

The sights and smells of the café brought back a wave of memories. All the carefree times she had hung out with friends here, without a worry in the world. Telling Ellison she was pregnant. She took a big breath before forcing herself to smile and walk over to Sherry. She had her long dark hair in a ponytail, and was dressed head-to-toe in name brand clothes. The only thing that had changed in a year was significantly more make-up.

"Hi Sherry," she set the stroller alongside the empty chair and sat across from her past in the form of Sherry.

"Oh my gosh!" Sherry bubbled, as she peaked around the hood of the stroller. "Is this your baby? He is *so* cute!" She sat down and leaned forward, "I can't believe you went and had a baby without telling us! You always were a bit of a quiet one!"

"Well, the last time I hung out with everyone you called a teenage mom a slut. So I wasn't exactly going to tell you…"

"Oh. Well, that's other girls! I wouldn't have called *you* that. But who's the dad? I didn't even know you were sleeping around!"

Jaz resisted the urge to roll her eyes. She wasn't interested in feeding the gossip chain. "That's between me, Alex, and the dad. No one else."

"Oh, right, Of course! Hey, did you hear I almost made the varsity volleyball at university? I was sooo close. But definitely next year. And our junior varsity team won everything, of course. I, like, did no studying all year. I mean, I passed and everything. But there's so much partying there! I had to take it all in, you know? What about you? Did you make varsity?"

"I was pregnant. I didn't go to university."

"Riiiight. So, what do you do now? Just hang out and play with your baby?" Sherry eyed Alex's stroller.

The waitress interrupted, and Jaz suddenly realized she was craving chili cheese fries. Sherry ordered a caesar salad and a milkshake. "I have to watch what I eat, you know. To stay in shape for varsity. Hey what brand is your shirt? It's super cool! Is it, like, Greek or something?"

"Sherry, we both went to Mandarin school together. You don't recognize it? Even just what it is?" Jaz knew her own Mandarin was pretty weak, but at least she could tell Mandarin from Greek!

"Nope! Looks Greek to me! Haha!"

Jaz started to hope their food would come quickly. She was ready to leave!

"Well, anyways. It's Mandarin. For momma. Alex is wearing a matching one that says 'baby'. I made them. It's part of the clothing line I started."

The waitress brought the milkshake and a glass of water for Jaz. Sherry reached for the straw and then stopped. "*You* started a clothing line? That's weird. You'll never make decent money then."

205

"Well, it supports me, plus an Executive Assistant and a bookkeeper, and five contractors. So I think it's doing OK." She tried not to gloat, but she was definitely proud of her business.

Sherry's mouth dropped open for a moment of blissful silence. But it didn't take long for her to catch her verbal stride again, "Where? Are they, like, in boutiques and stuff?"

"Just on Instagram. You can follow me, or the company. They're linked. And I have a lot of people that come in for personal shopping services." Jaz smiled to herself. Yeah, she was bragging. And it was fun.

Immediately Sherry pulled out her phone and started looking through the listings. "Holy cow, these are so cool! But they're all baby and adult clothes? Where's the stuff for us?"

Jaz resisted the urge to remind Sherry that she was supposed to be an adult too. Then, she flashed back to the day she got her first two followers in the maternity shop. Carrie acted like she had clothes almost ready to list, which forced Jaz to take action and start selling. With a silent prayer of thanks to Carrie, she leaned towards Sherry and beckoned her closer.

"It's still a secret," she whispered, "But the new line of clothing is going to be released soon. You are going to *love* the clothes. They'll be way more expensive than the stuff you see right now. Because it's pretty high end, you know?"

Wide eyed, Sherry nodded, "Don't worry, you can trust me. I won't tell a soul."

Jaz sat back and thanked her. She figured by the end of the day she'd have dozens of new followers who were all keeping Sherry's 'secret'. It was well worth a slightly awkward visit and the cost of a plate of chili fries.

Just before the food came Alex started fussing and Jaz picked him up, "Hey you," she cooed, "Enough time laying down, huh? This is Sherry." She pointed to Sherry, and Alex almost followed her finger.

"Uh, hi?" Sherry answered. With a baby in her sights she was unsure what do to next. The food arrived, and both girls started eating.

CHAPTER 37

*J*az walked quickly along the sidewalk to her parent's place, pushing Alex in the stroller. She'd worked late the night before on a new line of clothes she could market to people like Sherry, and then fell asleep while nursing Alex this morning. The last thing she wanted to do now was be late for lunch at her parents'.

They both answered when she rang the door.

"Jaz! Come on in! Here, let me help you with the stroller." Her dad lifted the front end of the stroller over the threshold and directed it into the entryway. Jaz followed in, and took her shoes off before picking up Alex and grabbing the diaper bag.

She followed her parents into the living room where there were some appetizers laid out on the coffee table. It was as if she was a guest. Maybe she was.

"Let me take Alex and you grab a little something to eat. Your mom made them herself!"

Jaz took a little plate and added a few things on it but didn't eat anything. "I'm too nervous to eat!" she blurted out, and then immediately regretted it.

"Nervous? Why are you nervous?" Her mom was taking careful bites from the food on her plate.

"I really want you guys to like me and Alex. But things are so different now."

"Jasmine. I think we handled your… pregnancy… badly. But that is no reason to have further trouble."

"Thanks Mom. I'd like us to be OK."

"Have any of your friends contacted you?"

"Yeah, Sherry did." Jaz relaxed a little, "We went to Connie's for lunch yesterday. It was strange. She hasn't changed. But I have."

"You've changed for the better. Your mom and I, we think you did the right thing under the circumstances."

Jaz felt a weight lift off her shoulders that she hadn't known she was carrying. "Thank you. That means a lot." She paused, "And the meeting with Sherry wasn't terrible. It gave me the idea to start a new clothing line directed at people like her. You know, people who pay anything to wear the right brand name?"

Her dad smiled, "Ah, if you get Sherry as a customer you can probably retire soon. I've never known anyone to shop like she does. Her dad and I golf together once in a while and her credit card bills are almost all he talks about."

"Wait, you golf?" She didn't remember her dad every golfing.

"Golf, walk, I even tried fishing!"

"Why?" It seemed so out of character for her dad, who had always worked late, come home and worked some more, and reluctantly gone to events when her mom insisted.

He exchanged a glance with his wife. She reached out and took Alex from him. Jaz was torn between watching how her mom would respond to Alex and giving her dad her full attention. He had already spoken more in the last few minutes than Jaz expected. Something was different about him—and maybe about her mom, too.

"When you…" he cleared his throat and started again, "The day you told us you were pregnant was quite a shock for me. Of all the things to happen, that was one that I desperately hoped you wouldn't have to go through. I went to work, but an hour later I got chest pain so bad that they rushed me to the hospital."

"What? Daddy! I'm so sorry!"

"It wasn't your fault Jaz. All the years of working long hours every day and the stress of work just caught up to me. It was just a minor heart attack, but it was enough to scare your mom and I."

"I felt like I lost you that day," her mom added looking up at Jaz, "The thought of losing your dad too was terrible."

"You know my dad died of a heart attack the year before you were born?" Jaz nodded, "Well, I realized that I was going down exactly the same path he did. And I didn't want that. So, with your mom's help, I changed some things."

"He only works forty hours a week now. No overtime, no weekends."

"And I don't bring work home either. We always ate healthy, but you know how much I don't like to exercise. So I try to do stuff I don't mind too much. I golf almost every weekend. And your mom and I go for a long walk every day."

"So that's why you walked to Lisa's last week!"

He nodded, "I've been feeling much better. The only thing missing from my life has been you. And now Alex. I also—your mom doesn't like this part—but I also went to see a counsellor. I knew my dad held everything in. I didn't want to do the same thing. It's been helpful."

"It is not a stranger's job to fix our problems." her mom stated with finality. Alex whimpered at her firm voice, and she softened her tone, "But she did help your dad. He has a lot to say now." She smiled at him, and Jaz marveled at how they had made their marriage work, even though she knew now that they weren't in love at the start.

"I kind of saw a counselor too," she said quietly. She kept her eyes on her dad so she wouldn't see the disappointment on her mom's face. "That day you kicked me out. I ended up at the clinic where I got the pregnancy test done. The physician's assistant—her name's Kara— she saw me in the parking lot after they closed, and she took me to her friend's house. That's where I stayed. At Carrie's. She was in the middle of getting her master's in counseling."

"You didn't go to your boyfriend's?"

"I didn't have a boyfriend. Just one night with a guy who thought I should have an abortion when I told him I was pregnant. I had nowhere to go, and Carrie took me in."

"Jasmine... I did not know... I thought you had lots of people to stay with."

"No. I didn't tell any of my friends. And then when you told Ellison's mom that I left for Europe on a gap year, and they were all messaging each other about it without asking me what really happened, I just deleted the app and tried to forget about them. My new friends are all a lot older than me. But they like me, and they've been there for me for everything."

The timer on the rice cooker beeped from the kitchen. "Let's go in and each lunch," her mom said standing up, "What does Alex need?"

"I fed him just before I came, so he should be fine. I brought a playmat that he can lay down on while we eat." She turned to the entry way to get it out of the bottom of the stroller.

"I can hold him. Do you have some toys or something for him to do?"

"Yeah, of course." She unclipped two toys from the strap of the

211

diaper bag. When she went to hand them to her mom, she was stopped.

"What's on your shirt?"

"You tell me Mom!"

"Oh, it's mamma in Chinese!"

"Yep, and look at Alex's!"

"Oooh, baby!"

"Something like that!" Jaz laughed.

Her dad was bringing dishes to the table, and he stopped to inspect the shirts. "I've forgotten so much. It's such a beautiful language."

"Where did you get these from? No stores I know, I am sure."

"I made them."

Both parents turned to her, shocked looks on their faces.

"You're proud to be Chinese?" Her dad looked confused, "But I thought kids your age just wanted to blend in."

"Not me Dad. And probably not a lot of others, either. We're proud to be different. To have parents and grandparents that worked hard to build a life here. I want to raise Alex to be proud of all the good things about being Chinese."

They sat down and started eating, her mom expertly balancing Alex on her knee while carefully eating. Jaz tried not to stare. She had never seen her mom holding a baby before.

"I'm going to do things different, too. About raising Alex."

"What do you mean?"

"Well, I tell him I love him all the time. And I'm going to let him try whatever he wants, without forcing him to do stuff. And he only has to go to university if he really wants to."

"But how will he make money Jasmine? You can't do that to him!"

"Mom, lots of stuff is changing. A good education is still important, but there are other ways to be successful. In less than a year, I've built a business that can support Alex and I and I'm doing what I love. Maybe he'll be able to do the same thing!"

"I've been in the corporate world my entire adult life and I don't know anyone who's done anything like what you've done. Starting a business from scratch that makes money in the first year? It's quite impressive."

"Thanks Daddy! And I'm just getting started." As Jaz began talking about her business, and her dreams for the future, Alex relaxed and fell asleep in her mom's arms. She held him, perfectly still, while Jaz talked about growing her business, helping others, and how hard it was for women who were trapped in bad living situations.

"Well," her dad began as they finished eating, "This is a very good thing you're trying to do. But your first priority must be to your son. And when it comes to these people you want to help, I do think education is the best investment."

"But how does that help a senior citizen?" she challenged.

"Jasmine, you should not talk to your father like that."

"I'm sorry. I don't mean to be disrespectful." She missed talking to Lisa and Maria, who welcomed different points of view without correcting her. "I *would* like to know what you think about how to help seniors" she added gently.

"They should live with their families" her mom stated firmly.

Jaz struggled with how to continue the conversation without offending her parents, and gave up. "Alex sure looks comfy Mom."

She looked down at the sleeping baby, "Does he sleep at night? A lady at the hospital has her daughter and granddaughter staying with her. She says the baby screams every night."

"No, he sleeps through almost every night. I think I've been pretty lucky. The other moms I know say Alex is easier than their babies were."

"Of course. It's because he's Chinese."

"Well, he is that." Jaz agreed.

Her mom looked at her sharply, "Is the father Chinese?"

"Yes," she replied, knowing where the conversation was going.

"Do we know him?"

"Mom, I really want to respect you here, but he asked that no one find out. And I agreed." She held up her hand slightly to hold off her mom, "I know there are times to break confidentiality, but I don't think this is one of those times. Alex is well provided for, and surrounded by people who love him—including his grandparents." She smiled, "That's all he needs right now."

Her mom sighed, "It is not right."

"Maybe not, but I think it's the best for now." Hoping to avoid having to directly contradict her mom, she got up. "I think it's time for me to head back. Thank you so much for having us over. Even the rice tastes better at your place Mom."

She started to clear the dishes from the table.

"Do not do that!" her mom said as sharp as she could without startling Alex.

"Nice try Mom. You sit there with Alex, and I'll clean up before I leave."

"But you do not know what to do!"

Her dad placed a hand on her mom's arm, "I'll help her."

The whole experience of having her dad help her clean up lunch proved to Jaz that things had changed between her parents. She enjoyed the quiet chatter with him while they worked, and soon everything was done.

Before picking up Alex, she gave her mom a gentle hug. Jaz could tell how uncomfortable she was, but at least she didn't stop her. She turned and hugged her dad next. "I love you guys!"

Then she gently picked up Alex. "Why don't I walk you home?" her dad suggested.

She looked at her mom, "Do you want to come too?"

"You go ahead."

They walked in silence for a minute before Jaz asked, "Do you have any more problems with your heart?"

"No, I've been pretty good. Your mom takes good care of me too."

"It's so weird to think your marriage was just an agreement to start with. You guys seem so happy now."

"We are. There were some very hard times. We always wanted to have one more child. But it wasn't to be. At least we have you. And Alex!"

"So, did you ever hear anything else about my birth mom?"

He sighed, "No. We closed ourselves off to that community. I could have handled the judgment against me, but it wasn't fair to raise you among people that would always see you in a bad light. I can give you her name if you like. But her family was very unkind."

"Maybe sometime. Not now though." They slowly walked up the path to the house. Jaz turned and hugged her dad once more. This time he hugged her back gently. "Bye Dad. Will I see you again soon?"

"Yes! Of course! Would you let us come take Alex for a walk once in a while?"

She beamed, "Of course! You mean without me, don't you?"

"Yes. Well, we want to spend time with you too. But we have some grandparent time to catch up on. Perhaps Tuesday at seven?"

"He'll be ready! Bye Dad!"

"Bye Jaz." He bent over the stroller where Alex was just beginning to wake up. "And bye to you little man."

Jaz opened the door with a light heart and a huge smile.

A NOTE FROM THE AUTHOR

A Note From the Author:

Thank you for taking the time to read *Heartwarming Designs*! If you enjoyed it, please consider telling your friends or posting a short review. Word of mouth is an author's best friend and much appreciated! Thank you again!

To be the first to hear when my next book comes out, and for a chance to win bookish prizes, sign-up for my newsletter:

www.carmenklassen.com

And you can like my Facebook author page:

fb.me/CarmenKlassen.Author

May all your days be full of good books, nice people, and happy endings.

Sincerely,

Carmen

READ ON FOR AN EXCLUSIVE SNEAK
PREVIEW OF BOOK 5...

*C*arrie sat at the table, her cup of coffee forgotten in front of her.

"So, let me try and get this straight." She looked at Jaz who was practically bouncing in her chair. "Your business is doing so good you have extra money..." Jaz nodded, beaming.

"And you," She turned to Maria who was in her wheelchair, "have some friends who need a different place to live..."

"Lovely people," Maria assured her.

Carrie turned to Lisa, "And you've done the math, and think this is possible?"

"Well, we've got monthly costs covered for a large house, yes. An apartment would be a bigger challenge. Not impossible though," she quickly added.

"I just can't... I mean, I'm all for helping people, you know that. But what you're suggesting is so..."

"Don't say impossible!" Jaz warned, "You'll get Lisa going all over again if you use that word!"

"What other word is there?"

"I like bizarre. Ridiculous is good too. And definitely use amazing. That works perfectly." Maria offered.

Carrie looked at the three women around the table. Had it just been nine months since she had dropped off a shy, pregnant Jaz to live with her quiet, hard-working friend and her mother? She laughed, "What *happened* to you people?"

Preorder Book 5: A Roof Over Their Heads

ALSO BY CARMEN KLASSEN

SUCCESS ON HER TERMS

Book 1: Sweet, Smart, and Struggling

Book 2: The Cost of Caring

Book 3: Life Upcycled

Book 4: Heartwarming Designs

Book 5: A Roof Over Their Heads (Preorder)

* * *

NON FICTION

Love Your Clutter Away

Before Your Parents Move In

Made in the USA
Lexington, KY
01 September 2019